A Soldier's Tale

A Soldier's Tale

Gary Taylor

CHARTRIDGE
BOOKS OXFORD

Chartridge Books Oxford
5 & 6 Steadys Lane
Stanton Harcourt
Oxford OX29 5RL
Tel: +44 (0) 1865 882191
Email: editorial@chartridgebooksoxford.com
Website: www.chartridgebooksoxford.com

First published in 2015 by Chartridge Books Oxford

ISBN print: 978-1-911033-00-4
ISBN ebook: 978-1-911033-01-1

Typeset by Domex e-Data Pvt. Ltd., India
Printed in the UK and USA

Also by Gary Taylor:

- *A Deal's A Deal*, 2007. ISBN 9781843344315.

- *Troubled Minds*, 2010. ISBN 9781907568435.

Foreword

By

Major Ian Constantine
Royal Horse Artillery

I must admit to being a little surprised to be asked to write this foreword; I'm certainly no literary expert, but I am a keen reader and probably more importantly in this case, a serving soldier. My son and his wife train under Sensei Gary Taylor and it was my son who approached me about Gary's new book; I didn't know what to expect but was very pleasantly surprised when I received the draft. The fact that 50% of the proceeds of this book are going direct to The Royal British Legion is reason enough for me to write this, but I'm pleased to say I thoroughly enjoyed the story as well.

I have been privileged during my thirty plus years in the Army to meet many Second World War veterans, including many airborne veterans from Arnhem and one thing that always stands out when you talk to them is their humility. This is something that Gary has captured in the character of Ernie White. Ernie's tale is one that could have come straight out of a Commando Comic Book, indeed fans of that genre will not be disappointed. I found it to be a real "page turner" and read the whole book in two sittings, pausing only for lunch.

I commend *A Soldier's Tale* to you and hope you enjoy it as much as I did and of course there is the added bonus that you are helping to support servicemen and women, from all conflicts, through the work of the British Legion.

It was nine o'clock in the morning, the date 11th November 2014. Ernest White, Chalky to his friends, sat at the living room table of his West Midlands home, deliberating over how many boxes of poppies he would be able to sell at the local supermarket after the Remembrance Day service. Each year he aimed to beat his previous year's record. The highest number of boxes ever sold by one person at his ex-serviceman's club was six. He placed the seventh box on the top of his pile thinking, 'this year the record's mine.' He had been fund raising for ex-servicemen for sixty years, which must have been a record in itself but, like so many old soldiers, that was the sort of man he was; proud to have served his country, no matter what it had cost him physically and psychologically. When war was declared in 1939 he had been the perfect age to join up and did so without hesitation, along with his two older brothers, Arthur and George. Now, at ninety four years of age, he was mentally sharp, but was slowed by injuries acquired during the war, which, over time, he had learned to live with.

Like so many ex-servicemen, Ernie was proud to wear his medals. He had so many, people would comment, 'Any more of them mate and you'll tip over.' He was amused and proud. As he lifted his jacket from the back of his chair, he carefully drew the sleeve of his shirt across the medals to give them an extra polish. His arthritic fingers struggled to maintain a grip on the collar as he raised the jacket towards his shoulder. The doorbell rang. With a deep sigh, he put the jacket back down and turned towards the hall. Stood at the front door with his hands clasped together, furiously blowing on them in an attempt to ward off the cold November air was his son, Steve, with twin twelve year old boys, Simon and Jason.

They were Ernie's only grandchildren. He was extremely proud of them and told everybody so, to the boys' embarrassment. 'Come on, Dad,' Steve said to himself, stamping from one foot to the other trying to keep warm. Simon pushed open the letterbox and peered through at his grandfather, making his way slowly and rather unsteadily towards him, quietly humming some non-specific tune to himself, as he always did.

'Here he comes,' said the lad, letting the letterbox spring shut. As the door opened the boys were in before the old man could step to one side.

'Careful you pair, you'll have your granddad over; he isn't as young as he used to be.'

The old man's wrinkled face beamed with pleasure. 'Don't worry Steve; I can still handle this pair if I have to.' He grabbed Simon's shoulder as he attempted to scamper past. The boy stopped immediately, knowing that his grandfather could easily topple over.

'See,' said the old man, thinking he had stopped the boy in his tracks, 'Go on, Rabbit.' It was the name he had affectionately used for the boys since they were very young.

'It's the big day today then Dad,' said Steve, closing the door behind him,

'Yes, I'll see if I can sell a few poppies down the shops later.'

He tried to sound as if it was nothing special but Steve knew better; it was all that had been on the old man's mind for the last fortnight.

'Fancy a cuppa son?'

'Thought you were never going to ask,' replied Steve.

The old man shuffled back down the hall, across the sitting room and into the kitchen, Steve following closely behind, constantly eyeing his father's every move, just in case he was to fall. He'd suggested a walking stick several times, but his father had stubbornly refused.

Steve watched while his father filled the kettle and, as always, warmed the tea pot. He always used the tea pot, even for a single cup, a routine insisted upon by his beloved wife and continued after her death. Steve admired his father's dogged independence but at the same time worried about how long it could last.

Jason had made a beeline for his grandfather's jacket; they only got to see his medals through the November Remembrance period, as they were usually locked in a wooden chest under his bed with his other wartime memorabilia. The boy slipped the jacket on, to his brother's amusement, raising his right hand in a salute and marching round the room; Simon laughed out loud.

Their father, annoyed by the rumpus in the next room, stuck his head round the door and, seeing the lad in his father's jacket, instantly saw red.

'Get that jacket off now!' he demanded, 'Wait till I get you home.' Sheepishly, the young lad slid the jacket from his shoulders and onto the back of the chair.

'Don't be hard on them, Steve,' said Ernie, passing his son a mug of tea, 'life's too short, they're good lads, they don't mean no harm.'

'Just keeping them in check Dad, exactly what you did with me.'

The old man nodded in agreement, picked up his own mug and followed his son into the sitting room.

Ernie was not much of a churchgoer but always attended the Remembrance Sunday service. The boys carefully placed the boxes of poppies in the boot of the car, while Steve helped his father on with his jacket. With great care, Ernie checked the alignment of his medals above his left breast pocket. He scanned the sitting room; on the table, impeccably brushed, lay his red beret. Slowly making his way to the table he picked it up and with great precision, positioned it firmly on his head. After checking his reflection in the mirror above the fireplace, he turned to his son.

'Looking good Dad,' said Steve, knowing how much it meant to him. Ernie appreciated his son's words, but he knew otherwise. As he glanced in the mirror, he was only too aware that his once bright blue eyes were now pale and rheumy and the red beret that once sat proudly on a head of thick, brown hair now covered nothing more than a few wisps of grey.

'Come on, let's get you down to the church; your old mates will be wondering where you are.'

'Right you are son,' replied Ernie, his back appearing a little straighter after putting on his beret.

It was only a short journey in the car, no more than ten minutes. Every year Ernie attended the Remembrance service and every year there would be another face missing. As they pulled up outside the church the old man began to wonder who it would be this year. Steve checked his watch, 'Right on time Dad.' The service began at 10:30am and finished promptly at noon. Steve got out of the car and went round to the passenger side opening the door for Ernie, who swung his legs out a little gingerly. The boys were already out and running along the pathway leading to the steps at the church door.

'Take your time Dad,' said Steve, 'another couple of minutes won't hurt.' His father had a reputation for being punctual and even at his ripe old age he wasn't going to let that reputation be tarnished. It was a struggle up the steps but Ernie's determination and pride kept him moving. Steve held the door open and Ernie's back straightened as he stepped inside. In the pews on the left hand side of the church stood a number of ex-servicemen, all wearing their regimental berets and headdresses, and numerous medals, each one equally proud of their regiment or corps. As Ernie shuffled past keeping as tall a posture as he could, one by one they acknowledged him. Some nodded, others said, 'Good to see you, Chalky,' or simply 'Ern.' The majority just smiled, happy to see that the old man in the red beret had made it to another Remembrance Day.

As usual, it was an emotional service, stirring up old memories that would never really be put to bed. The local Territorial Army unit laid a wreath of poppies then, finally, everyone respected the two-minute silence; each and every old soldier left with his own thoughts for just one more fraction of time. Leaving the church, Steve held on to his father's arm to steady him, not wanting an accident at the top of the steps. The vicar stood at the main door and shook the hand of every one of the ex-servicemen as they shuffled or were wheeled past, and of the remainder of the congregation.

Once Ernie was in the car all that was now on his mind was his pitch.

'Ready, Dad?'

'As I'll ever be son,' replied Ernie, struggling to clip his seatbelt in. Steve reached over.

'Let me get that.' Quickly, he clipped it in and looked behind him to the rear seats.

'Ready, lads?' They both gave a thumbs up. Without another word, Steve clicked the central locking button and pulled out into the traffic, extending his right arm out of the window to thank the driver of an oncoming car for letting him go.

It was a short journey to the shopping centre where Ernie had arranged to set up his pitch. Steve pulled up as close to the main door as he could; the less his father had to walk the better. As the boys took the boxes out of the boot, Ernie climbed out of the car, straightened his jacket and beret, then very slowly followed the boys towards the entrance. A small table and a chair had already been placed just inside the door. The boys positioned the boxes on the table and pulled the chair out from under it for their grandfather to sit on.

'Looks busy today, Dad,' remarked Steve, 'you might just break that record yet.'

'Fingers crossed son, fingers crossed.' smiled Ernie, pulling the lid off the first box of poppies. Once everything was in place, Steve rounded up the boys, who were becoming a little too mischievous for his liking.

'Right Dad, I'm taking these two scallywags home before they get into trouble. I'll be back later to see how you're getting on.'

'OK son, see you later. No need to hurry, I've got all afternoon.'

'Bye Granddad!' called the boys in unison as they headed towards the door.

Ernie sat patiently. He had never been one for pushing the poppies under people's noses; he preferred the offer of a little charity to be given freely. Still, it was going well, with a steady stream of people giving their change and occasionally a generous individual would drop a couple of pound coins in the box. After about half an hour, a tall, well-built man, who Ernie thought to be in his mid-thirties, approached the table. He had neat, short black hair and an equally well-groomed moustache.

'I couldn't help but notice you were in the Para's.' Ernie loved it when people showed a genuine interest, rather than just feeling obliged to put money in the box.

'Yes,' replied Ernie, 'ten years in all; stayed on after the war.'

'I was in the forces myself, served in the Gulf and Bosnia. Served for nearly the same time as yourself, give or take a few months. Threw it in for the missus in the end. The name's Alex.' He offered his hand and Ernie reached up and shook it.

'Pleased to meet you Alex, I'm Ernie, Ernie White.' Alex felt in his pocket for his wallet and picked up a poppy. 'You want a pin?' asked Ernie, pulling one from a card on the table.

'Yes please, Ernie.' Once he had fixed the poppy onto his jacket, he took out a ten-pound note, folded it over twice and slipped it into the slot on top of Ernie's collection box.

'That's very generous of you.' said Ernie.

'It's nothing; I wish I could afford more.'

Alex gazed at Ernie's medals, 'I bet there are one or two stories behind all those medals, Ernie.' Ernie pulled his chin in to look down at his medals,

'One or two, some I haven't told a soul about for fifty years or more.'

'I'm all ears Ernie, I love a good tale, I have a few myself.' Alex looked around the foyer and spotted a chair by the disability vehicles. 'Two ticks, if you don't mind the company, I'll get that chair and have a sit with you for a while.'

'Feel free,' replied Ernie, pleased at the unexpected opportunity to talk about his medals and meet another ex-serviceman, albeit of a younger generation. Alex fetched the chair and sat next to Ernie. 'I'm intrigued now Ernie, do you remember what they were all for?'

'Every one of them,' said Ernie, proudly.

'I recognise a couple,' said Alex, pointing at the medals. 'The green and orange ribbon, circular one, that's a campaign medal, the Defence Medal.' Alex looked pleased with himself.

'That's right,' said Ernie.

Alex continued 'The one next to it, that's the Victory Medal.'

'Some call it that,' said Ernie, 'but its real name's the War Medal.'

Alex's eyes were drawn to one medal in particular. 'Gosh Ernie, is that George V on that one? The blue and red ribbon?' asked Alex.

'DCM,' replied Ernie. Alex's eyes widened, 'My God, Ernie, you have a Distinguished Conduct Medal?'

Ernie made no response other than to simply raise his eyebrows a little.

'Where did you earn that?' asked Alex, in awe.

'Arnhem,' Ernie replied.

'You were at Arnhem Bridge?'

'Not exactly,' said Ernie, 'you see, we got towed over in gliders, landed about eight miles from the bridge.' He paused for a moment. 'I lost more friends on that first day than most people lose in a lifetime.' Ernie slowly lowered and shook his head.

Alex could sense the emotion and did not want to upset the old man. 'It's ok, Ernie, if you don't want to talk about it.' Ernie raised his chin, his eyes glistening slightly.

'Suppose it can't hurt it; was a long time ago, but the funny thing is I remember it like it was yesterday.'

It was a Sunday morning, September 17th 1944.

'Come on Chalky!' Came a call from the back of the canvas-covered truck.

At five feet eight inches, Ernie White was a wiry, powerful young man. He climbed up onto the backboard and flipped his legs over the top to join the others in his section, being careful not to drop any of his precious kit. The convoy of trucks had already loaded up a good part of the 1st Airborne Division. Their mission had been kept a closely guarded secret for some time but now, literally a few hours before lift-off, each and every soldier knew just how important the success of this mission was. The Dutch bridges, strategically placed over the Rhine and other nearby rivers, had to be taken and held. If successful, it could dramatically reduce the length of the war by increasing the advance of the Allied forces.

The 1st Airborne had been kept in reserve during the D-Day landing and the waiting around had made these ferocious, yet extremely professional soldiers ready and eager for action. Ernie's company were a closely-knit bunch of lads, his own section even tighter. They had all seen action at first hand and each trusted the man next to him with his life. As the trucks pulled away the rear of the vehicles fell into silence, each man left with his own thoughts. Some busied themselves by checking their weapons or sharpening knives but, if the truth were known, even the most battle hardened were somewhat fearful of what lay ahead of them.

The trucks arrived at an undisclosed airfield somewhere in the south of England. The tailgates were unfastened, kicked down and, two or three at a time, the troops leapt from the back of the vehicles.

'D'ya want a lift down Jacko?' teased Ernie. Jack Hawton, Jacko to his mates, was a six foot three inch Birmingham man who stood no nonsense from anyone.

'If you don't move Chalky I'll jump straight on top of your head, short arse.'

The banter from the men was constant, but always in good humour. On the airstrip a line of Handley Page Halifax bomber aircraft and Hirsa gliders were stood one in front of the other, already coupled to each other and ready to go. Ground crews were carrying out final checks; operation Market Garden was about to begin. The gliders would go in first followed by the parachutists, and the heavy equipment vehicles would then reinforce them once they had secured their objectives. Ernie's platoon had been chosen to go in on gliders, not their favourite means of transport, but orders were orders.

Once the men and their equipment were loaded, the Halifax engines burst into life and the tug cables on the Gliders were checked. It was now just a matter of waiting for the command to go. The men of the 1st Airborne had simply to sit tight, put their faith in the skill of the pilots and hope to God that the Luftwaffe and the German ground to air defences were having a bad day.

The Ministry of Defence expected that once the German air defence cottoned on to the operation, there would be something in the region of thirty to forty percent aircraft loses, a statistic the men were better off not knowing, so stealth and secrecy were essential for the success of the mission.

Ernie and his platoon were tightly packed, sitting side by side, with their equipment in every available nook and cranny. Flight duration was approximately three hours twenty minutes, which meant they should be there round about one pm. When they were near to the landing zone the glider tug cables would be released. Then it was a matter of the pilot getting them down on the ground as quickly and safely as possible. The Allies believed that enemy defences in the area were very poor. However, unknown to them, Germany had recently sent two divisions of the 1st SS Panzer Corps into the area to practice scenarios on how they would deal with an airborne assault.

Finally, they received word to go. 'This is it chaps,' the pilot called out.

In front of the glider, the Halifax's engine speed picked up and the aircraft slowly began to move away. The slack on the cable attached to the glider was quickly taken up and, as it pulled taut, the glider jolted forward. There was no turning back now and, as each of the aircraft picked up speed, the men anxiously anticipated the familiar feeling that they were airborne.

One hour into the flight the men were becoming restless, the cramped surroundings and apprehension of what lay ahead taking its toll. Some tried to close their eyes and lose themselves in sleep but it was futile. A Scottish lad, Jordan Campbell, turned to Ernie and asked in a soft Highland accent,

'What do you plan to do after the war Chalky?' Ernie looked him in the face; not yet twenty years old and further away from home than he had ever been. He didn't really want to know Ernie's plans, it was just a nervous attempt at conversation to try and take his mind off things.

'Not really sure, having a few beers with my brothers would be a good start though.' They both smiled then fell silent, Jordan absent-mindedly gnawing his nails. Ernie reached out and squeezed his arm, 'Hey,' the young soldier looked up, 'it'll be alright.'

Jordon took a deep breath and forced a half smile. 'Course it will,' he replied, 'bloody cake walk.'

Just on two and a half hours into the flight, over the throb of the Halifax engines drawing them towards their destination, they became aware of the sound of anti-aircraft flak. Over the next few minutes it became louder and louder; unnervingly close.

'It's going to get a bit bumpy from now on,' shouted the pilot. Hirsa gliders were not designed to take hits from any kind of weaponry, let alone 88mm anti-aircraft guns. The flight path that wing command had chosen for the squadrons of planes avoided areas of concentrated flak. When it did happen the accompanying fighters soon took out the positions. With over 850 support aircraft, the Luftwaffe decided not to attack the huge squadron of planes.

As they approached the glider release points, the aircraft began to reduce in height. The anti-aircraft guns were too close for comfort; explosions shook the glider to the point where some men thought they were done for. As the formations of Halifaxes and gliders continued reducing height some were not so lucky.

A direct hit on one of these relatively fragile aircraft was devastating for its occupants. The mood of quiet tension and restlessness transformed to one of fear and panic as the pilots of both the Halifaxes and the gliders witnessed horrific sights; gliders literally being cut in two, their pay load of gallant soldiers falling helplessly to their death. The troops, windowless, could only imagine the scene from the yelled commentaries of the glider pilots and the dreadful sounds surrounding them. From somewhere towards the rear of the aircraft, Ernie heard one of his comrades singing, or rather shouting above the noise, the words of a familiar song.

'Glory, glory, what a hell of a way to die!' It was a song adopted by some of the Allied airborne forces as a kind of ice breaker in dire situations. Another voice joined in, then another and another, until they were all singing at the tops of their voices.

At the correct altitude and position, the pilot of the Halifax radioed to the glider to prepare for cable release.

'This is it lads,' called the glider pilot, 'we're going in.'

Ernie's platoon glanced apprehensively at each other. This was the most dangerous part of the flight; their lives well and truly in the hands of the glider pilot. Through the large screen, the pilot watched as the released cable plummeted downwards. As he took control, he could already see the landing zone some distance ahead. They were a good twelve kilometres from Arnhem, so didn't initially expect a great deal of resistance upon landing. It was to be a totally different story for the men parachuting in, with many not even making it to the ground before being sprayed with light machine gun fire from soldiers of the Waffen SS, a highly professional section of the German infantry.

The pilot could clearly identify gliders on the ground as he made the approach. Soldiers on the ground were already securing the perimeter of the landing zone. Happy with the approach, the pilot descended, 400 feet, 300, 200. The men braced for landing; you only got one chance in a glider. As the tyres hit the ground a deep sigh of relief passed throughout the aircraft. It was a short, very uneven strip but the pilot had it under control. Before the aircraft came to a complete stop the men had already secured their kits and had weapons at the ready. Who knew what was waiting for them outside? The door opened and without any hesitation the men leapt from the aircraft, their eyes searching every corner of the field for potential threats.

More gliders arrived, one or two less smoothly as some parts of the landing strip were rougher than others and it was just a matter of luck which line you took. The majority of the injuries sustained were minor, although some sustained banged heads and a few had broken limbs, but that wasn't going to stop what was quickly becoming the biggest airborne landing the world had ever seen. Ernie and his platoon were given the north edge of the landing zone to secure and take up defence.

Once the officers and senior NCOs had been finally briefed and given their orders they would start the advance towards Arnhem.

'That must have been one hell of an experience Ernie, not knowing what to expect as you jumped out of that glider.'

'It was,' replied Ernie, 'but nothing like what would happen in the next few hours.'

Ernie's eyes widened and he slowly shook his head from side to side as he recalled the events that followed. 'We got sent on a recon mission, just a small section of us, twelve men in all travelling light. You see, there had been some talk about tanks in the area, Panzers. Well, we hadn't got any heavy firepower, that was all due to follow, the few Jeeps we had were reconning the main routes to Arnhem. So we set off on foot just before two.'

The advance to Arnhem had been divided into three main routes; Leopard, Tiger and Lion. Ernie's section had gone slightly off the beaten track, north of Leopard route. It wasn't meant to be more than a couple of hours' reconnaissance mission. Then, once they reported back with their findings, they would join up with the main battalion.

'Keep off the path and stay inside the tree line lads,' instructed Sergeant Mills, 'stay sharp and space out, single file. Chalky, take point.'

Sergeant Mills, Geordie to the other senior NCOs, had been given command of the section. Prior to his military career he had worked in the mines; his huge thick set muscular frame was a testament to a hard working class background. He was a highly respected and battle hardened soldier who had a reputation for sorting things out behind the billet with his fists should anyone question his authority.

They had been walking for almost an hour, cautiously crossing open ground and taking great care not to be seen from the roads. All signs of their comrades had been left well behind. Fortunately, there had been no sign of any enemy tanks or threats that needed quickly reporting back to HQ. In the distance, about a mile east of their position, was a series of farm buildings.

Mills studied his map with two other NCOs. Once they had agreed their plan of action he called the men in. 'Listen in, we're going to make for those farm buildings,' he indicated the location on the map, 'Once we've secured the buildings, it's defensive positions. Got that?'

They nodded in unison.

'Right, let's get moving.'

The approach to the buildings was very slow and convoluted. Not wanting to leave themselves exposed to ambush, they avoided the open ground, which doubled or even tripled the distance to the farm. At last, about one hundred yards away at the back of a large barn, Mills dropped onto one knee and signalled his men to spread out in a line. He pointed at Ernie and then Campbell. They knew exactly what he wanted. They were both to advance while the section covered them.

With safety catches off and their weapons held firmly in front of them, Ernie and Campbell approached the wooden doors, rushes of adrenalin making their stomachs feel as if they had just eaten something they shouldn't have. Ernie put his back to the wooden door. The plan was for him to pull the door open and if there was any sign of the enemy inside, Campbell would let them have it. In the distance the rest of the section looked on vigilantly. Without making a sound, Ernie nodded his head and shaped with his mouth; 'three, two, one...' Quickly, he pulled the door open. With his weapon at shoulder height, Campbell dashed through the door scanning every corner of the room, Ernie following closely behind. As they ran through the building the adrenalin in their bodies reached new levels, surging through their veins. The barn was empty. Breathing heavily, Campbell turned to Ernie,

'What a rush.'

'Know what you mean,' replied Ernie, clicking the safety catch back on his weapon.

Campbell went back to the barn door and waved towards the section. Two at a time, the men advanced to the barn until they were all safely inside. As instructed by Mills, they took up defensive positions at strategic points within the building.

Mills turned up the volume on the radio. They had maintained radio silence up to now, not wanting to risk drawing any attention unless absolutely necessary. While the men passed around a small ration of chocolate, Mills tried to contact HQ. All he was getting was interference,

'God damned radio,' he hissed, swotting the radio with the palm of his hand. He wasn't exactly sure how far they had walked but, clearly, it was out of the radio's range. The type 68 hand-held radio sets were not designed to carry a signal over five miles and this distance was greatly reduced by the combination of built-up areas and patches of dense woodland.

Private David Hughes was keeping a close watch on an area of woodland around four hundred yards away. His name had prompted the nickname of Taffy, which had followed him throughout school and into the military, even though he had been born in Walsall, spoke with a broad Black Country accent and hadn't a Welsh bone in his body. There was no breeze and everything appeared still. Then something caught his eye. His body tensed. Instantly, his senses sharpened as he carefully examined every shape, trying to focus within the darker spaces between the trees. Then he saw it again, a glint of something metallic; maybe it was the lens of a sharp shooter focusing in on their position. That wasn't for him to decide. Keeping as still as possible, he softly called out,

'Searge, movement seen, ten o'clock.' The entire section went on red alert. Mills clicked off the radio and, keeping low, he moved swiftly over to Taffy's position.

'What you seen Taffy?'

'Just inside the tree line Searge, can't be sure but twice I saw something flash, like something metal.'

They both strained their eyes scanning along the edge of the wood and spotted them almost at the same time; German infantry. As they appeared from the trees they kept low. There were possibly twenty of them, heavily camouflaged, probably doing a similar reconnaissance mission. Mills had to think fast. They were outnumbered but by the way the Germans were advancing they hadn't seen them, so the element of surprise was in their favour. On reconnaissance missions the usual action would be to back off without being seen and report their findings. Unfortunately, the open land behind them meant that backing away and disappearing wasn't going to happen. Before they reached even half way across the open fields the German foresights would have been trained on them. The only option was to hide and hope they walked straight on by. If they didn't, there was going to be one hell of a firefight. Mills quickly surveyed around the building. Above them was a hayloft covering the full width of the barn.

'Right lads, up in the loft pronto. Taffy, keep your eyes on them till everyone's up top.'

One by one they clambered up a rickety old ladder that had been nailed to the side of the barn, Taffy finally bringing up the rear.

The loft was deep, dark and well stocked with hay. Mills peered through a knothole; the Germans were fifty metres from the building. As quietly as possible they cocked their weapons.

'Quiet now lads,' whispered Mills, 'no itchy fingers.'

Lying very still, with their senses at an acute level of anticipation, they waited for the sound of the door opening. Fingers crossed, after a quick glance in the building they would walk straight on past. The sound of the door creaking open set all their hearts pounding. The muzzle of a very curious StG 44 assault rifle appeared at the edge of the barn door. Stealthily and with great caution a German soldier entered the barn, closely followed by one of his comrades. Unlike Ernie and Campbell who had dashed into the barn with guns raised, the Germans tiptoed in trying not to make the slightest noise.

Glancing across at each other in the hayloft the British soldiers could hear the Germans whispering to each other in their native tongue. Not being able to understand what they were saying heightened their senses even more. What they had actually said was 'It looks clear.' One went back out to signal his commander while the other stood very still, listening for the slightest sound. His attention was drawn to the ladders and his eyes followed them up to the hayloft. As he put his foot on the first rung of the ladder, Mills drew in a large albeit silent breath. One rung at a time the German climbed the ladder. Mills was the closest to him, although well hidden by a large bale of hay. The soldier's head came level with the loft floor and he peered through the gloom for anything out of the ordinary. He saw nothing, just hay. As he started back down the ladder, the sound of a slight rustle in the hay brought him to a halt.

He remained motionless, listening. Mills looked across to where the noise had come from. Burrow, a young private, had made the small movement that may well have given away their position, and was only too aware of the possible outcome. The German started back up the ladder and climbed into the hayloft, slowly making his way towards the bales at the back, where the men were hiding. Mills quietly but quickly slid his dagger from its sheath. As the soldier approached, with lightning speed he leapt up and closed a hand around the German's mouth. Almost instantaneously the cold steel of his dagger thrust into the side of the German's neck. As blood gushed, more by luck than judgement, the blade severed the man's spinal cord between his third and fourth vertebrae. Death was instant. Without as much as a chance to cry out the soldier collapsed in a heap. His lifeless body was dragged in behind the bails and once more there was silence.

No more than thirty seconds later his comrade came back into the barn. He had done just as Ernie and Campbell had; waved in the direction of his comrades giving them the all clear to advance towards the barn. It seemed that a confrontation with the main force was now inevitable. One by one the clicks of safety catches being released could be heard in their small confined area. The lone soldier called out to his friend, 'Nickolaus?' He stood very still in the eerie silence. Each man could hear his own heart thudding in anticipation of the forthcoming battle. The heavily camouflaged German soldiers arrived at the barn to find their brother in arms standing frozen, looking up towards the hayloft.

Mills was closest to the front of the loft and listened carefully; the more of the enemy that came into the barn, the better. Clasped tightly in his right hand was a grenade. He had already removed the safety pin. The more they could take out before the firefight, the more chance they had of winning it. Mills looked straight across the loft. Crouching low and looking directly back at him, Taffy's eyes were filled with fear. Mills tried to reassure him with a smile and a wink then threw the grenade out of the loft towards the German soldiers. Some took cover; others raised their weapons in an instinctive attempt to defend themselves. The British soldiers tucked their heads in and waited for the explosion while Mills kept a close look out in case one of the Germans threw it back into the loft. The next moments were complete and utter hell.

The grenade landed at the feet of a young German soldier who tried to pick it up to throw back in return but, in his panic, he fumbled. He took the full force of the blast. Before the smoke cleared the barn was engulfed in automatic weapon fire. Mills was the first into them. Knife in hand, he leapt from the top of the hayloft straight onto three German soldiers. One raised his weapon; the muzzle forced itself into Mills' midsection and the gun went off point blank, a gaping exit wound opening up on his lower back. Still he slashed and stabbed at the soldiers trapped underneath his huge frame. Others joined the mêlée, some firing from the loft, others jumping from height onto their enemy. In this kind of combat there were no rules of engagement. A German soldier lobbed a grenade into the hayloft. Chalky saw it land but couldn't get to it in time. He turned and attempted to dive behind a large hay bale to shield himself from the blast, but was halted by an excruciating pain in his neck that spun him around and BANG. It was as if everything around him exploded.

Ernie lay at the top of the hayloft, in what seemed complete silence. He could see Campbell sitting on top of a German, bludgeoning his head with what looked like the stock of a broken weapon. Mills was laid flat on his back, two or three bodies underneath him, his lifeless eyes staring blankly at the barn ceiling. Ernie tried to get to his knees. One leg wouldn't respond but as he struggled to get to his feet, out of nowhere, an unseen force hit his shoulder, throwing him backwards to the rear of the loft. Then everything became dark.

'Blimey Ernie,' said Alex, 'I take it you were shot?' Ernie nodded, gradually returning from that dark place to the supermarket foyer.

'Twice,' he replied, 'neck and shoulder, and the blast from the grenade broke my leg and left a couple of nasty pieces of shrapnel behind. You'd expect it to have been a lot more painful, not that it wasn't, but the truth is I didn't know much about it. There was so much going on around me I never had time to think. Adrenalin was pumping through my body, next thing I blacked out.'

Alex was enthralled by the story unfolding before him.

'Well, what happened next?' he asked, leaning towards Ernie with his elbows on his knees, keen for the next instalment. Ernie rubbed his chin and gazed into the middle distance as his mind wandered back.

Ernie slowly regained consciousness. As his mind cleared he wondered where he was; soon, reality hit home. There was complete silence. For a moment, he thought he might be dead. He tried to focus in the greyness around him and could see thick swirls of dust moving gently in shafts of sunlight. He began to recognise the barn, realised that he was in the hayloft, and was then aware of an acrid smell and the bitter, metallic taste of sweat, dirt and blood on his lips. As he turned his head to the right, the agonising pain in his neck and shoulder quickly confirmed that he was very much alive. He could move his right arm but it was very painful, and his breathing was restricted. His uniform was covered in blood, how much of it was his he didn't know. Lying all around him were men from his unit, or what remained of them. Then he remembered the grenade and diving for cover.

The men directly in front of him had taken the main blast, shielding Ernie from certain death. Struggling to his knees the pain in his right leg was so severe he thought he was going to pass out again. He had to get help. He awkwardly and painfully pulled himself up against a bale of hay and looked over the edge of the loft. What he saw made him feel sick; a mass of dead men. Both sides had fought literally to the last man, and he was the only one left alive. He listened: silence. Not even the faintest sound of movement or breathing. He slumped against the hay. What was he to do?

Suddenly, the silence was broken by the sound of an engine some way off. Struggling to the other side of the loft, he peered through the gaps in the boards. In the distance, some half-mile away he could see a half-tracked vehicle with a large roof-mounted machine gun, flanked by at least a hundred, maybe a hundred and fifty men; German infantry. This must be the main force the reconnaissance squad had been dispatched from, just as his group had been. If they caught him he was done for, especially with his injuries and what had happened to their comrades. He had ten or maybe fifteen minutes at most, and desperately scoured his surroundings for somewhere to hide. But, even if he were successful in hiding from them, he would probably die of his wounds. There was only one thing for it, and he had nothing to lose.

Ernie crawled over to the body of the first German soldier Mills had killed in the loft. They were a similar build. Ernie noticed the small skull insignia on the dead soldier's collar. Waffen SS. No wonder the battle had been so intense. Just like Ernie's outfit, this was a crack infantry unit, not renowned for being the friendliest of adversaries, and another hundred plus soldiers were minutes away. As quickly as he could he removed the soldier's uniform, the thought of being taken or worse hastening his progress. Fortunately for Ernie, the approaching Germans were just as cautious about the barn and outbuildings as his own men had been, a caution heightened by the sound of gunfire they had heard not an hour before.

The soldier's uniform was covered in blood, and the limpness of his body and his own injuries made it difficult to strip the man. But it was a matter of life and death and that thought alone spurred Ernie on. He pulled the soldier's I.D. tags over his head, the caked on blood making it impossible to see whose identity he was taking. He pulled on one of the soldier's boots, reached down to the other, but the pain from his leg injuries was so severe he almost cried out. It was partially on, and that would have to do. He was desperate, his hands shook and his eyes burned with sweat from his forehead; every movement seemed to be taking forever. He used his knife to roughly and clumsily tear at the trouser leg somewhere near his own injuries, then heard German voices.

He wanted to put his uniform on the German but there was no time. He dragged his own I.D. tags over the soldier's neck and covered him with hay; it would have to do. Ernie crawled to the edge of the loft and with his good arm and leg, positioned himself on the ladder. He had to get down before they came in. Taking his weight with his good arm, he hopped down one rung, then another. He tried to pull his injured leg in towards the ladder and on to a rung to take some of his weight, so that he could get a better hold, but it was too much. The boot, only partially on his foot, slipped through the rungs, jolting his injured leg against the side of the ladder. Excruciating pain shot through his body and the feeling of nausea overwhelmed him. Everything began to spin. Losing his grip he tumbled towards the pile of bodies, his broken body unconscious before he hit the ground.

In silence the Germans approached the barn, just as the British patrol had done. Four men keeping low cautiously ran up to the main door, using any means they could to peer through the gaps in the timber construction. They could see the bodies, some grotesquely entwined, some with limbs missing, and others covered in blood from the gun and grenade battle that had taken place. Realising it was now more of a mausoleum than a farmyard barn they pulled the door open. Weapons at the ready they walked inside, the lead German soldier called out in his native tongue just in case anyone was still alive.

'The building is surrounded. Stand up!' He knew it was futile but it had to be done. They waited for a few seconds, nothing, he turned to one of his comrades, 'Tell Hauptsturmführer Schrader that it's all clear.'

After scouting round the building and securing the immediate area they began checking the bodies. First they started separating their own comrades from the enemy. Ernie now semi-conscious heard the German voices. He began to groan to attract attention. One of the German soldiers stopped in his tracks.

'Quiet, everyone.' They all stopped what they were doing and he scanned the pile of bodies surrounding him. 'I'm sure I...' again Ernie groaned. The German spotted him.

'Over there!' he pointed, quickly scrambling over to Ernie. 'He's one of ours. Medic, quick! Hold on my friend, we've got you.'

Ernie opened his eyes and the German smiled down at him.

'You're a hero my friend, they'll give you a medal for this.'

Ernie had no idea what the soldier was saying. The medics quickly assembled and began working on him, with Ernie slipping in and out of consciousness. A wound that had gone straight through his shoulder didn't appear life threatening. They were more concerned with an entrance wound in his neck that must have been a ricochet; it would need surgery and fast. His boots were removed and trousers cut off, revealing an open fracture and some nasty shrapnel entrance wounds. The leg was splinted; it would also need immediate surgery. They placed him on a stretcher and the last that Ernie remembered was an injection in his arm. After that, everything became dark.

In all the confusion and haste to give medical treatment, the tunic, trousers and boots that Ernie had been wearing were discarded, so that the fact that there were no bullet holes in his tunic or that the shrapnel holes in his trousers did not match injuries, was completely overlooked. After all, he was a hero. For the next twenty-four hours all Ernie remembered was the sound of German voices and the constant use of a name: Nickolaus.

Whenever he felt his body being lifted, or bounced around in a vehicle the pain would surge and he would lose consciousness. Occasionally he tried to cry out, but it was like the worst sore throat imaginable. For now, thankfully, his voice was completely gone.

After what seemed a lifetime of sleep he came round. He was lying in a bed with a large amount of padding around his neck and right shoulder. Also, there appeared to be a frame under the sheets covering his hips and legs. He glanced around the room; it looked like a stately home with high ceilings and ornate plasterwork. The windows were almost ceiling height, allowing plenty of light to enter. The building had probably been commandeered as the Germans had advanced across Europe, turning it into a makeshift hospital. There were eight beds in the room all occupied by men, presumably injured soldiers, some bound in bandages from head to toe. Thinking about it, Ernie realised he wasn't far off that himself. A nurse came into the room holding a tray.

Beginning on the far side of the room, she went from bed to bed placing what looked like a small paper cup on each soldier's bedside cabinet. As she reached Ernie, she stared straight at him. She looked about fifty years old and her hair was obviously dyed, as it didn't match her complexion. Her shoulders were back and she walked ramrod straight, exactly fitting Ernie's image of German woman. Speaking in German she asked,

'Are you fully awake Nickolaus?' There was that name again thought Ernie, but he had no idea what she was asking. He opened his mouth to show that he couldn't speak and raised his hand to his neck. She intervened by reaching out to stop his hand. 'The stitches aren't healed yet, and it will be sometime before you get your voice back. The doctor will explain when he does his rounds. Now, take your medication.'

Ernie hadn't got a clue what she was saying. She picked up the paper cup and gave it to him in his good hand. The penny dropped. Medication, thought Ernie. He put the tablets in his mouth and she gave him a glass of water, as he swallowed he screwed up his eyes and grimaced, it was so painful it was like trying to swallow broken glass.

'That's normal with what's happened to you,' she said. 'Now rest.' Still oblivious to what she was saying, Ernie simply laid back on his pillow. She continued dispensing medication to the other beds. Ernie lay there following her with his eyes. He would have to bide his time and just concentrate on recovering, but he realised that in his condition, it could take some time.

Later that day two men in white coats moved from bed to bed closely followed by the same nurse, it was the ward round. Ernie watched them. He considered pretending to be asleep but he had to face the music at some point, so it might as well be now. He'd have to reveal his true identity. They moved towards Ernie and began to look through the charts on the clipboard that hung at the foot of his bed. The elder of the two doctors balanced a pair of wire-rimmed spectacles precariously on the end of his nose, his eyes darting from charts to patient.

'So, Rottenführer Kesling, you are back with us.' Ernie just stared up at him, unaware of what was being said. 'You have been sedated for the last three days. We needed to give your body every opportunity to rest. The injuries you sustained were very serious and I don't mind saying, it was touch and go. But you are a strong young man and now it seems quite a celebrity. I have been instructed to put you in your own room and take exceptional care of you.' The doctor raised his eyebrows, 'I have a feeling you are going to have one or two high profile dignitaries visiting you when I tell them you are well enough. For now you must rest.'

The doctor scribbled something on the charts and hooked the clip board back over the bottom of Ernie's bed, before turning to the nurse.

'Make sure Rottenführer Kesling gets the first available private room, and that new nurse,' hesitating, he clicked his fingers in frustration, not able to remember her name. The nurse assisted him. 'Nurse Keller, Herr Doctor?'

'Yes, that's the one,' he replied, 'she is to be assigned to his room until he is well enough to have visitors.' He turned back to Ernie and smiled over the top of his spectacles,

'We wouldn't want anything to happen to such a high profile patient in our care now, would we?' With that he moved on to the next bed.

The following morning, Ernie had eaten what felt like shards of glass for his breakfast. Two orderlies came over to his bed, waffled out a couple of sentences in a language that he thought might be Dutch, then proceeded to unfasten the locks on the wheels of his bed. He hadn't any personal belongings as such so, with a man at each end they pushed the bed out into the centre of the room and spun it around to face the door. A little concerned with what was going on, Ernie raised his hand to the man at the bottom of the bed as if to say, 'what are you doing?'

'You're being moved to a private room sir,' said the orderly. Which didn't help much, as his language sounded more complicated than German.

Down the corridor and through a large reception room, Ernie started to get a feel for the building. It was definitely some kind of stately home. Every now and then he would catch a glimpse of the grounds through a window. The lawns and flower beds seemed to go on forever and were immaculately manicured; somebody obviously took great pride in maintaining the place. Finally they stopped at a large ornate wooden door. Very awkwardly but with great care not to hit the bed against the beautiful woodwork, they steered the bed into the room. Ernie looked around; it was what his family would have called 'very posh.' A large desk stood in front of a French window, the far wall was covered in leather bound books, and in front of it an oversize, much-worn chaise longue that in less troubled times had seen many a relaxed reader. The room was still very sparsely furnished, much too big for just one bed. Placing the bed in a position that gave him a nice view out of the windows. The orderlies locked down the brakes on the bed, nodded to Ernie, and left the room.

Ernie, still unable to leave his bed, lay and waited. Thirty or forty minutes went by, then he heard a knock at the door. He couldn't call out even if he was capable. After about thirty seconds, he saw the door handle turn. A very small but extremely beautiful face came around the edge of the door; things are looking up, thought Ernie.

Nurse Trudy Keller came into the room and closed the door behind her. Her long blonde hair was tightly plated and pinned to her head; at just nineteen years old she was everything the so-called Aryan race was supposed to be. With sparkling blue eyes, golden hair and an athletically toned physique, no one would ever have guessed the secrets she held close to her heart.

Her real name was Ruth Zimmerman, the daughter of a rich Jewish businessman. Her father had anticipated the Nazi uprising and arranged to have false documents made for his only child, declaring her an orphan and breaking any ties with the Jewish community. He knew the way things were going it was just a matter of time before all Jews would come under scrutiny, with Germany's worsening economic decline. Soon it would be every man for himself, so he had started to hide his wealth abroad, but it was getting harder and harder to do so. At least with his daughter's looks she could easily fit into the new regime. From the age of fifteen she had been in a school for young ladies, paid for by an anonymous beneficiary, himself, of course. She was registered at the school as having no next of kin. Sending her away was the hardest thing he had done. It had broken both his and his wife's heart, but it had to be done. Just over twelve months after she had been at the school, letters from her benefactor had stopped. She was sick with worry, but following her father's orders precisely had kept her true identity a secret, even from her closet friends. Unknown to her, both her parents had perished at Auschwitz. Her mother had been gassed on arrival and her father had been worked to death over a period of a few months. Only days before the Nazis came for them her father had managed to wire enough funds to the school to take care of his daughter's fees for the foreseeable future. After that she would be on her own.

She hadn't been told much about this soldier she had to attend to, only that he had been very badly wounded, was SS, and a hero. SS alone to her was bad news, she thought of them as Hitler's bullyboys, which some of course were. But the front line Waffen SS infantry divisions were amongst the best the German military machine had to offer, professional soldiers in every sense of the word.

Sheepishly she approached Ernie, avoiding direct eye contact. She said,

'Good morning sir.' Ernie managed to understand such a basic phrase and nodded in return, pointing first at his neck then at his mouth. 'You can't speak,' she said, Ernie just stared.

'Well I guess I will have to do all the talking for us.' As she smiled Ernie felt mesmerised by her beauty. She didn't even like giving German military the time of day, but if the Nazis won the war she had to secure some kind of future. Her policy since being separated from her parents had been, keep your friends close and your enemies closer; it was safer that way.

Over the next weeks, Ernie's affection for the young nurse began to grow. Sometimes she seemed a little distant with him, but the language barrier was always going to make it a problem. If the truth were known, she was actually starting to like him also. His facial expressions and mannerisms were kind and gentle. All the things she had heard about these so-called SS bullyboys didn't seem to be evident in this man. But there was something about him she couldn't quite put her finger on. Maybe that was what attracted her.

Now able to walk, albeit painfully and with sticks, Ernie's rehabilitation was coming on in leaps and bounds. When alone he tested his voice. Slowly it was coming back, a little scratchy and sore but improving. He now had to be very careful not to accidentally say 'please' or 'thank you' when normal good manners were required.

The young nurse had been literally left at his beck and call. Most mornings when he awoke, she would be sat in the chair by the window in his room, either drinking coffee or just staring out into the grounds watching the arrival of another day. Some days he would have flashbacks to that day in the barn. The doctors had done as much as they could for the injuries to his body, and a good job they had done; now time would be the great healer. Psychologically he would probably never completely heal. On this morning in particular it felt as if he was reliving the whole experience. In his dream he called out to his comrades as the grenade was thrown in their direction: something he never had time to do when it actually happened.

'Take cover, take cover,' he said over and over, only now he was talking out loud in his sleep. The young nurse turned, she had seen him having nightmares before but this was a first, she had studied languages at boarding school and had a fairly good grasp of English.

The more he twitched and turned the louder he called, 'Take cover, take cover.' Nurse Keller quickly got up and moved over to his bed. Placing her hand across his mouth she gently shook him. For a moment he seemed to fight waking up, then suddenly he woke with a start. His eyes where unnaturally wide, she could see fear in them, he realised why she was staring at him so intently.

'You were talking in your sleep,' she said, there was an uncomfortable silence. 'I don't understand, why where you speaking in English?' Ernie knew the cat was out the bag.

'Are you going to report me?' She sat on the edge of his bed.

'Why would I report you, am I missing something?' For a moment Ernie thought he had got away with it.

She looked confused then the penny dropped. 'That's why you never talk and always look confused when the doctor talks to you, you can't understand him, you're English.' Quickly she got to her feet and backed away,

'Are you a spy?'

Ernie laughed, 'A spy, do I look like a spy?'

'I don't know I've never seen one.'

'I can promise you I'm not a spy, and I certainly wouldn't hurt you,'

'Are you sure?'

Ernie smiled, it seemed to relax her a little.

'Sit down,' said Ernie, 'I'll explain what happened.' Nervously, she clasped her hands together and moved back to the bed, sitting uneasily on the edge. Over the next hour or so Ernie explained what had happened to him and his section. If he hadn't done what he had he most certainly would have been killed. It was a matter of life or death and he chose life. The more she listened the more she understood the position he had found himself in. Without giving too much away about her own personal circumstances, she told him of her feelings for the Nazis who where currently ethnically cleansing her country. She wanted to tell him everything, but felt the time wasn't right.

After their long conversation she agreed to help him conceal his real identity. It would have been easier just to turn him in, but there was something about this man; an affection that was growing with every day she was with him. Letting her heart rule her head was dangerous. Only time would tell the outcome.

'You were lucky there, Ernie.' said Alex, sitting back and stretching out his arms.

'She was a great girl my Ruth,' said Ernie, 'I wouldn't have had a chance without her, she risked everything for me, like the day I got measured for my new uniform,' a grin appeared on Ernie's face, 'I remember it like yesterday.'

Every day at one pm an orderly would bring a tray with Ernie's lunch. With the current situation in Europe he wondered where they got all the sumptuous food. There were always fresh vegetables and either chicken, pork or fish; it seemed there was no expense spared for their so-called war heroes. Ernie was sat eating his lunch when a knock at the door alerted both of them. Now that Nurse Keller was aware of Ernie's language problems she always tried to speak first with any visitors he had. She walked over to the door, and with her hand on the handle she turned to Ernie. He raised his eyebrows and nodded, a deep breath and she opened the door. There was an elderly man stood in the hall with what looked like a suit of clothing draped over his arm.

'Good afternoon, I have been sent to complete the final fitting of Rottenführer Kesling's new uniform.' Nurse Keller moved to one side to let him enter. 'Thank you,' he said bowing his head. He marched in with the athleticism of a man half his age, and with a slightly over-exuberant smile on his face went straight over to Ernie.

Again he placed his feet together and bowed,

'Rottenführer Kesling, my name is Wolfgang Stein it is a great honour to meet you, I have heard a lot about you. I am sorry to interrupt your meal sir, I have been sent to check the fitting of your uniform. Would you prefer if I came back later? It will not be a problem.'

Ernie looked straight at him. He needed help, and hadn't got a clue what the man had said. Nurse Keller stepped in,

'Herr Stein, would you like to leave the uniform and come back for it a little later?' With that he pulled the cover off the uniform.

Ernie realised what it was all about. He placed his knife and fork down, pushed the chair back, and grabbing his stick and with one hand on the table he stood up. He pointed at the uniform, and gestured for him to hand it over.

Again Nurse Keller intervened.

'Rottenführer Kesling cannot talk at present Herr Stein, due to his injuries sustained fighting for the Fatherland.' Stein held out the uniform and bowed apparently in awe of one of his country's heroes. Ernie took the uniform, walked over to his bed and placed it on the top cover. It wasn't like the uniform he had taken from the dead soldier. It was a lot grander, almost like some kind of ceremonial dress. Ernie noticed the small sculls on the collar, which identified him as SS. Deciding to go with the flow he started to undress and put it on. Nurse Keller quickly moved over to help him. It was a little big in the shoulders, and the sleeves were long but on the whole a good fit.

Stein took a small metal box from his inside his jacket pocket, opened it and placed it on the table. Then he proceeded to stick pins in the shoulders and sleeves.

'Perfect,' said Stein, 'it will be ready in two days, I will inform your superiors.'

Ernie just stared at him and accepted whatever he had said. Nurse Keller helped him take off the uniform. Stein put the uniform back in its cover, being careful not to pull out any of the pins. Again he bowed and bid them farewell.

Every evening since Ernie had been back on his feet, albeit with the aid of his sticks, Nurse Keller would take him out into the gardens for a slow walk. It was hard and the pain in his leg meant he had to sit down on benches at regular intervals. Even with the pain it was the highlight of his day. On this particular evening they walked silently in the moonlight, occasionally exchanging a shy smile.

'May I call you Trudy?' asked Ernie.

She thought about it. Ernie thought maybe he was being a little too formal as she went very quiet. Then she turned to him and said,

'No, but you can call me Ruth.' Ernie looked confused. With that she told him everything about her secret life, her family and the boarding school where she had spent so much time worrying day after day about her parents. It felt so good talking to someone, like taking a huge weight from round her neck. Ernie was dumbstruck. What were the chances of them meeting? They both agreed it was fate. They could find a way through it if they worked together.

That night she never left his side. She pulled the chair just feet from his bed and sat looking at his silhouette in the darkness before falling into a deep sleep. Ernie lay awake for hours contemplating how they could escape. With his current state of health it seemed futile. There was no way he could go on the run, and if he did, what would happen to Ruth if they caught up with them? They had to stay quiet and hidden. According to Ruth, in two days' time when the uniform came back they had something planned for him. Maybe an opportunity would present itself. Only time would tell.

The next morning after breakfast a letter was delivered to Ernie's room. He nervously he opened it, and after a quick glance he passed it to Ruth. As she read it the concern on her face was obvious to see.

'Well?' asked Ernie anxiously waiting to know his fate. Without raising her eyes from the letter she said, 'They're sending you back to Germany.'

'How can they send me back?' said Ernie, 'I've never been there.'

Her eyes darted from the paper. 'Don't joke Ernie this is serious. It says an escort will collect you at nine tomorrow morning and take you to a secret military location within the Fatherland. A member of the medical staff will accompany you to assist with any physical problems or medication. If there are any special requirements for your existing conditions please forward them via the chief medical officer so arrangements can be made upon your arrival. It's signed by a General Blumentritt, he sounds very important.'

She folded the letter and held out her arm to pass it back to Ernie. As he took it their hands touched just briefly. Without making eye contact Ernie said,

'I hope it's you they send with me,' all the humour now gone from his voice.

'Me too,' said Ruth. It felt a little uncomfortable but instinctively they both had the urge to hold each other tight. Ernie pushed the letter into his pocket and gingerly took a step forward putting his arms around her. She reciprocated.

It was the first real human contact either of them had had for a long time. No words were said or needed. The feeling was more than just a friendly reassurance. It was a deep sense of togetherness, which was blossoming into a loving relationship. Ruth raised her head from Ernie's shoulder and for a split second their eyes met. Then they kissed. Their lips melted together as one, like the most natural thing in the world.

'So this was the girl of your dreams then, Ernie,' said Alex, trying to contain a cheeky smile.

'She sure was,' replied Ernie, oblivious to Alex's expression. 'I thought that was going to be the end of it when the uniform came back. I was told to be ready to leave at nine o'clock prompt the following morning. If it wasn't for Ruth's quick thinking that would have been it.'

'Why? What happened?' asked Alex, intrigued.

'Well,' said Ernie, shuffling on his chair to get comfortable, before continuing his story.

The package containing Ernie's uniform arrived the night before his departure. Herr Stein brought it personally just in case any minor adjustments were required. He knew that wouldn't be the case, but being the perfectionist he was, and the fact that he had been told it would be displayed in front of top brass, he wasn't taking any chances.

In Ernie's room Herr Stein proceeded to take the uniform from its protective cover. Beautifully pressed and impeccably presented, Herr Stein held it out like a piece of art.

'Rottenführer Kesling, I hope it is to your satisfaction?' Ernie couldn't understand his words but the man's actions spoke for themselves. Ernie raised his thumbs and nodded his head up and down a couple of times. Just then there was a knock at the door, Ruth quickly moved towards it, but before she got there the door opened. Two men entered. Ernie recognised one; it was the doctor with the ridiculously small spectacles balanced on the end of his nose that had dealt with his injuries when he first arrived at the hospital. He never did get his name, which was a shame, as one day he would have liked to thank him. The second he didn't know. He was a tall man in a sharp suit, greased back hair and a moustache Hitler himself would have been proud of. It was difficult to judge his age, but thirty to forty would have been a conservative guess. The doctor spoke first,

'Good evening Rottenführer Kesling,' he turned to Herr Stein. They nodded to each other. 'It appears you will be leaving us tomorrow. I have just received confirmation that your escort will be here to collect you at nine o clock in the morning.' Ernie just stared at him, inside he was thinking, 'shit, shit what do I do now?' Ruth acting on her instincts knew he was in trouble.

'Rottenführer Kesling was just about to try on his new uniform.' The tall man in the suit glared at Ruth with a look of, 'who asked you to speak?' Ruth picked up on it very quickly, lowering her head in a submissive gesture.

'Rottenführer Kesling still can't speak sir, his voice has not returned after his neck injury.'

'Yes,' said the Doctor, 'that is very strange, all your other injuries have healed well and I can't see any problems with your throat'. The tall man continued starring at Ruth and she felt herself trembling.

'Still,' said the doctor, 'time is a great healer, I'm sure it will return soon.' Herr Stein held up the uniform, 'If you don't mind sir, may we?'

'Yes yes, sorry for interrupting your fitting, I just brought Herr Eichmann to introduce to Rottenführer Kesling. He is overseeing the presentation the day after tomorrow.'

Herr Eichmann stepped forward put his heels together then raised his arm in a Nazi salute. 'Heil Hitler, it is a great honour to meet you Rottenführer Kesling.' Ernie nodded feeling very awkward.

'If I may sir?' said Herr Stein again holding up the uniform.

There was a dressing screen in the corner of Ernie's room with a chair behind it. Herr Stein extended his arm in its direction. With the aid of his sticks Ernie slowly made his way over to the screen went behind and sat on the chair. Herr Stein hung the uniform on the back of the screen and began to help Ernie remove his clothing; Ernie unbuttoned his trousers and tried to shuffle them down, something he still had trouble with due to the limited movement and pain in his right knee.

As Stein tried to help, Ernie grabbed the side of the chair in pain. He wanted to cry out but was worried what he might say. Stein could see he was doing more harm than good.

'I am sorry sir,' said Stein, 'I think it best I get your nurse to help you dress.' With that he went back round the screen his face said it all, 'Nurse, I think you have more experience of Rottenführer Kesling's injuries than I.'

Ruth quickly went behind the screen. In German she said out loud,

'Herr Kesling, please let me,' then in English she whispered, 'Stand up.' Within a few minutes she had him dressed. As he stepped from behind the screen Stein immediately began brushing off his back and shoulders with the palm of his hand. Ernie looked in the mirror on the back of the screen. He couldn't believe that he was stood there in a Nazi uniform.

Chapter 7

'First class job Herr Stein,' said Eichmann, 'a credit to your profession.' Stein smiled and humbly bowed his head.

'I think under the circumstances it would be a good idea for Rottenführer Kesling's nurse to accompany him, at least until after the presentation.' Ruth felt her heart rise. 'Can that be arranged Herr doctor?' The doctor looked a little disgruntled, he was already running a seriously under staffed facility. Ruth felt she had to strengthen her case; it was risky speaking out of line but necessary.

'Herr Kesling's injured knee and thigh require careful manoeuvring, it still gives him great pain when not attended to correctly.' The tall German again looked down his nose at Ruth. He paused for slightly longer than necessary, and Ruth felt herself shrinking in front of him.

'Right then, well that's settled,' said Eichmann, 'a staff car will be outside at nine in the morning. With that I will bid you a good evening.' Again he banged his heels together and raised his arm in a Nazi salute; Ernie with sticks in both hands just nodded his head. As the three men left the room the doctor turned his head, with distaste in his voice said, 'Take good care of our patient Nurse Keller.'

Feeling a little brash she replied, 'Certainly Herr Doctor, you can count on me.'

The rest of the evening was a little sombre, the apprehension of what the next day would bring was weighing heavily on both of them. Trying to stay positive, neither of them broached the subject, but they knew the next twenty-four hours could be the most dangerous of both their lives.

They both woke early the next morning. Ruth had hardly slept at all, her conscience getting the better of her. Was she doing the right thing? She could just carry on at the hospital, see the war out with her new identity and opt for an easy life. Whichever side won she could just blend back into society. Equally as quickly she would think of the fate of her parents, most likely sent to a concentration camp and executed just because of their ethnic background. Nazi scum, she thought to herself. This man she had spent the last couple of months with, he was so kind. Even with all the pain he had endured, he never once lost hope that he would be returned to his homeland. No, she knew why she was doing it. Ernie on the other hand never doubted her. She had already done more for him than he could ask of anyone, let alone a young girl he barely knew.

They ate breakfast just before eight o'clock, then Ruth helped Ernie dress in his new uniform. It was just before eight forty-five. Another fifteen minutes and the car would arrive. Ernie stood up straight without his sticks. He could actually cope without them now but to keep up the pretence, whenever anyone was around he would lay it on a little. He looked at himself in the mirror then slowly turned round to face Ruth.

'Well?' he said.

'You look very smart,' replied Ruth, 'not very keen on the SS badges but still, can't have everything.' He stepped forward and held her in his arms.

'Listen, if it all goes wrong, they will be none the wiser about you, just deny any knowledge that you knew I was English.' She held him tight.

'It's not going to go wrong.' Quietly they held each other until Ernie broke the silence.

'Right then, let's go, chin up.' Ruth smiled and he kissed the end of her nose. Ernie picked up both of his sticks and they set off down the corridor.

They had only been at the main entrance for one or two minutes when the sound of approaching vehicles caught their attention. Two BMW R75 motorbikes with sidecars both equipped with machine guns came roaring up the drive. Between them a Mercedes 170V staff car with its long sweeping front wheel arches and big round frog eyed headlights. The black paintwork gleamed in the sunlight. Obviously no expense spared for their heroes.

The staff car parked right outside the main door. The motorbike riders kept their engines running, toying with the throttles to the displeasure of the main entrance orderly. The driver of the Mercedes got out and came up to the entrance door; he was a young man no more than about eighteen years old, probably fresh out the Hitler Youth. Ernie and Ruth noticed straight away he wasn't SS, probably just a driver tasked with collecting them. It didn't matter either way, he was still the enemy as far as Ernie was concerned. Ruth opened the door. The driver smiled and stepped inside, he immediately came to attention towards Ernie and raised his right arm.

'Heil Hitler,' Ernie's sticks were a great excuse not to return the salute. As usual he nodded in response. 'Rottenführer Kesling, I have been sent with orders to take you to a secure location.' Ruth quickly intervened,

'Rottenführer Kesling is unable to speak due to an injury to his throat sustained in battle.'

The driver suddenly realised he was staring at Ernie's legs and sticks. He quickly averted his eyes back to Ernie's face. Always the gentleman, Ernie smiled understandingly.

'Forgive me sir,' said the driver, a little embarrassed by his actions. Turning round he held the door open for Ernie and Ruth to step outside. Once out he quickly stepped round them and opened the rear door of the car. Ernie stepped forward overdoing his disability a little more than was required.

As he ducked his head into the car he was engulfed in the smell of new leather. It was easily the most luxurious car Ernie had ever been in and probably ever would again. Ruth sat beside him and moved his sticks to the side, while the driver shut the door, came round the vehicle and got in. Looking in the rear view mirror the driver said, 'It's a long journey so please make yourselves comfortable, there are drinks in the centre console, anything else you need please just ask.'

'Thank you,' replied Ruth.

As they pulled away the motorbikes took up position in front and behind the car. Ernie looked out the back window; both the driver and soldier in the sidecar wore goggles. Their faces beneath looked like stone, no hint of expression. Their black uniforms, although not as fancy as Ernie's, bore the SS insignia on the collar. As he turned back he caught Ruth's eye, she smiled then raised her eyebrows as if to say: no turning back.

As the morning wore on they travelled through sometimes picturesque countryside, then the next minute war torn communities with barely two bricks standing on top of each other. They had been travelling for well over an hour when the driver partially turned round and said,

'We have to stop for fuel, I have been given a pre-arranged location, they will be waiting for us. We will stop for approximately fifteen minutes; if you would like to stretch your legs, feel free.'

Ruth smiled at the driver and said, 'Thank you we will take advantage of that.'

'You are welcome, about another five miles and we will be there,' he turned back to his driving. Ernie just stared at the back of the driver's head, oblivious to what the conversation had been about.

Fifteen minutes later the lead motorbike turned off the road and the staff car and rear bike followed. Ernie glanced around with an expression of concern on his face, but Ruth quickly picked up on the fact that he couldn't understand what the driver had said to them just a few minutes before. In an attempt to reassure him she placed her hand on the back of his and smiled. It seemed to work, as he sat back in his seat and accepted what was happening. The staff car came to a halt and suddenly out of nowhere they were surrounded by German soldiers. The driver wound his window down, and what must have been the officer in charge came up to his window and saluted,

'Heil Hitler,' the driver responded with the same salutation. The officer looked in the back of the car and nodded towards Ernie, he returned the gesture. 'Follow the road down the path and you will come to an opening, you'll see the fuel vehicle, they will fill you up.'

The driver thanked him, wound up his window and moved on. After about fifty yards they came to a clearing. On the far side a canopy covered lorry with the tailgate down was waiting. There were two soldiers; the one standing on the back of the lorry passed jerry cans to the other who placed them on the floor in neat lines. The staff car pulled up alongside the lorry. Without any prompting the soldier picked up a tundish and Jerry can and preceded to fuel the car.

'You can stretch your legs now if you wish,' said the driver, 'but don't go too far, I will give you a call when we are ready to go.'

'Thanks,' said Ruth as she reached for the door handle. Ernie caught on what was happening and followed her out of the car.

It felt good to straighten up, Ernie's leg and back had stiffened. As he stretched he heard his joints clicking. It felt good even if it was only for a few minutes. With the use of his sticks they walked over to the edge of the compound. Until Ruth felt sure they couldn't be overheard. 'They are filling the car up with fuel then we will be on our way. The driver still hasn't said where he is taking us but I have a hunch there is still a long way to go.'

Ernie nodded in agreement, after a quick glance around he said, 'You know at some stage we are going to have to make a run for it.'

Ruth looked anxious. 'I think we should wait till at least after the presentation or whatever they have in store for you. If we go before then it will attract too much attention and that's the last thing we need.'

'I agree,' said Ernie, 'wherever they take us, just stay close to me.'

Ruth held on to his arm, gently she rubbed it in an attempt to show affection without making it obvious. Turning to look at the car she muttered under her breath, 'Don't worry, something is telling me we are going to get through this.' Not wanting to sound negative Ernie gave no reply but thought, 'God I hope so.'

The driver leaned into the car, tooted the horn, and raised his arm. Ernie returned the gesture, 'Here we go,' said Ernie under his breath. They walked over to the car. Once secured the driver waved towards the officer that had directed them. The motorbikes with their heavily armed sidecars took up position front and rear of the car, and the small convoy speed off back towards the main road.

Once back on the main road, the driver reached over the front passenger seat and picked up a box, slightly smaller than a shoe box. Glancing behind he offered it over the seat,

'I managed to acquire some rations when we stopped, it's not a lot and I'm sure there will be plenty of nourishment at our destination.' Ruth saw the opportunity and took it.

'Where is it we are going, if I may ask?'

The driver hesitated for a moment almost unsure if it was safe to divulge the information. Then he said, 'Potsdam.'

Ruth nodded her head, 'That's not far from Berlin.'

'That's right,' said the driver, 'the Sanssouci Palace.'

'Gosh,' said Ruth taken aback, 'that's supposed to be a very beautiful place.'

'I wouldn't know, I have been to Potsdam a few times but never sightseeing,' replied the driver. 'Should be there in about two hours, that should be plenty of time before the presentation.'

Still trying to get as much information off him as possible Ruth asked, 'Who is giving the presentation?'

'Sorry I can't answer that, it's been kept very secret, but it must be someone very important. Maybe a high ranking general. Anyway, you both get some food inside you and try to relax. It's going to be very busy when you get there.' With that he took his eyes off the mirror and concentrated on keeping a safe distance from the lead bike.

Ernie stopped talking, and for a moment he appeared lost in thought.

'You OK Ernie?' asked Alex a little concerned by the old man's sudden silence. Just as if someone had flicked a switch in Ernie's head, he looked up.

'I'm fine thank you, I was just remembering that day.' He shook his head slightly. His expression was difficult to decipher, his eyes appeared to be smiling while the rest of his face seemed astonished by his own thoughts. Slowly the old man reached into his inside jacket pocket and pulled out another medal. Ernie held the medal in the palm of his hand and raised it up towards Alex.

'What the hell,' said Alex, 'that's an Iron Cross!' Ernie nodded.

'Do you mind if I hold it?' asked Alex with an air of excitement in his voice. Alex meticulously examined the medal. 'This is the real McCoy.'

'I know it is,' said Ernie, 'apart from my family you're the only person that has ever seen or held it in over sixty-five years, with the exception of Adolf Hitler.'

Alex raised his eyes. He felt like laughing, but his respect for the old veteran kept him in check.

'Hang on now Ernie, you're telling me, as a British soldier you were decorated with an Iron Cross for valour by Adolf Hitler in 1945?'

Ernie stared straight at him, his face totally expressionless. Alex suddenly became aware that his own mouth was wide open.

'Close your mouth son,' said Ernie, 'I know it's hard to believe, that's why I have kept it to myself for so long. As sure as I am sitting here it's true. What happened that day is as clear as if it was yesterday. We arrived at the Sanssouci Palace just after two in the afternoon.'

'Hello,' said the driver a little louder than needed, his eyes searching the back seats via the interior mirror. Ernie and Ruth had both fallen asleep; slowly they had slid sideways on the back seat into a more comfortable position. Ernie woke first, alarmed by the German voice coming from in front of him. Quickly he regained his senses and switched on to his surroundings. Gently he nudged Ruth who sat up with a start.

The driver smiled though his mirror, 'A little more refreshed now I hope, we are nearly there: five minutes.' Rubbing their eyes and yawning almost in unison they both attempted to straighten their clothing.

'There seem to be a lot of military vehicles around,' said Ruth to the driver.

'I told you, security is as high as it gets. I have a feeling you are in for a hell of a surprise.' With that, the driver concentrated on the road. Ruth looked at Ernie and raised her eyebrows. Ernie just stared back, still oblivious to the conversation.

All around were the signs of Allied bombing. Potsdam, being very close to Berlin, had sustained some intense bombardments. The Sanssouci Palace, once summer home of the Prussian King Frederick the Great, in its six hundred acres of magnificent gardens and vineyards, had not been exempt. Fortunately, the majority of the palace was still intact. Up ahead they noticed a roadblock, the driver slowed down. Two soldiers approached the car. The driver pulled down his window and handed the guard a folded document. He said nothing, just scanned his eyes over the paperwork. Like he had all the time in the world he looked at the driver then slowly directed his eyes to the rear of the vehicle. His eyes met Ernie's with a stare that was a little too long for comfort. Then he nodded towards Ernie and said, 'Heil Hitler.' Ernie nodded back and the guard stood away from the vehicle, gesturing to the soldier on the barrier to open up. He gave the driver back his document and they drove on. Ruth felt the tension building up inside her, and squeezed Ernie's hand.

As they approached the palace they noticed what appeared to be a large windmill. The war had certainly taken its toll on it but it was still standing, just. Either way it looked strangely out of place high up behind the stone walls of the palace. The security presence was now immense, small but heavily armed squads of soldiers where running to and fro, apparently all with a task to achieve in double time. There were a number of staff cars parked a little way up the road, each one with an armed guard. A soldier with a machine gun fastened tightly across his chest raised his hand and beckoned them towards him. They moved forward and he directed them into a space near the end of the line. After applying the brake the driver turned off the engine and quickly jumped out of the car. As Ernie reached for the door handle the driver beat him to it sharply pulling the door open and standing to attention. Ernie eased his legs out, overemphasising his injuries. As he stood up for a split second he almost said thank you, but more by luck than judgement his throat was so dry he just croaked and swallowed hard. The driver nodded respectfully. Ruth passed him his sticks and climbed out to join him. The soldier that had directed them into the parking space came from the other side of the car stood to attention.

'Rottenführer Kesling it is a great honour.' Ernie noticed the soldier also wore the insignia of the SS on his collar. 'Your heroism precedes you within our regiment.'

Ruth knew Ernie was again in trouble and once again squeezed his arm. Ernie picked up on it, and nodded and smiled at the soldier.

'Please, if you will follow me I will escort you to the reception room.' The soldier immediately set off in the direction of a large stone archway. Holding on to Ernie's arm Ruth gave him a slight shove. Ernie quickly understood what was required of him and followed the soldier, once again over exaggerating his ailments. Ruth held on to his arm making it seem that he couldn't manage without her. If they were separated he wouldn't have a chance. At least this way if she could direct him; they might just pull it off.

Realising he was moving too fast for the semi-disabled war hero, the soldier stopped before the end of the passageway.

'My apologies for rushing you sir,' again Ernie just smiled. The soldier held his out his arm and directed them into a room on their right. As they walked through the door, the full extent of why it was called a palace hit them. The ornate architecture of the walls and ceilings was magnificent. It wasn't a huge room but the amount of light coming through the long arched windows to their left gave the room depth and height. Just inside the door was a table full of charged champagne glasses, and a young girl, no more than about sixteen, dressed in black and white waitress attire held out a tray of drinks. Ruth took a glass for him and smiled at the girl.

Still holding on to Ernie's arm they moved forward, the escorting soldier led the way towards two large doors. Holding both handles he pulled the doors open. Ernie and Ruth both felt their stomachs drop. The room was again not massive but equally as magnificent as the last and was full of high ranking officers and dignitaries. This is it, thought Ernie, we are done for. He felt the eyes of everyone in the room zooming in on him, and then an elderly man in a sharp black suit came rushing over.

'Good afternoon sir, may I assume you are Rottenführer Nickolaus Kesling?' Ruth squeezed his arm once and Ernie nodded. 'It's a great honour to meet you, my name is Gerbert Huber I am the manager of the palace estate and here to make sure everything goes to plan. If there is anything you need do not hesitate to ask.'

Ernie raised his hand to his throat, Ruth interrupted,

'Herr Huber, excuse me but Rottenführer Kesling is still unable to speak or stand for very long.' He looked straight at Ernie,

'My apologies sir,' he clicked his fingers and a waiter was there instantly. 'A chair please, quickly.' The waiter dashed off and was back within seconds with a chair, which he placed by a window and ushered Ernie over to it. Ruth took his sticks and gave him the glass of champagne. Once comfortable Ernie sipped on the champagne, a drink he had never had the pleasure of trying. Over exaggerated he thought to himself. 'There are quite a few sons of the Fatherland being honoured today,' said Huber looking very pleased with himself, 'also we have another surprise for you.' Ernie just kept sipping the champagne hoping he would grasp something within the conversation. 'Your parents are on their way from Berlin.'

Ruth suddenly squeezed Ernie's shoulder so tight he flinched and spilt his drink down himself. Huber jumped back, 'My that did surprise you.' Again he clicked his fingers and a waiter appeared out of nowhere with a cloth and a fresh glass of champagne and started patting down Ernie's uniform. Just then, three or four high ranking officers walked through the door. Huber spotted them straight away, 'Excuse me sir, when your parents arrive I will send them straight over to you.' He bowed down as he backed away, the next party of dignitaries firmly in his sights.

Ruth had to talk to him; she leaned close to his ear.

'You need the toilet.' Ernie looked over his shoulder and shook his head. She took a deep breath and leaned down again, 'No, I said you need the toilet.' Ernie caught on. Ruth went over to a waiter and asked for directions. Once again laying on his injuries Ruth helped him to his feet and followed the waiter's directions. Ruth pushed the door open, and Ernie went in, it was more like a large bathroom than a toilet. Ruth glanced around the corridor, followed him in and locked the door. 'Your parents are coming.' Ernie looked a little dumfounded, 'I'll rephrase that, the parents of the soldier you are impersonating are coming and they will be here soon.'

Ernie's face said it all, 'We have to make a run for it now.'

'But how?' said Ruth. 'The place is swarming with security; we wouldn't get 100 yards past the front gate.' Ernie now completely forgetting about his sticks walked round the bathroom banging his fist on his forehead. 'Think, think, think,' he said out loud. Suddenly he stopped and turned to Ruth. 'We'll just walk straight out the front door and keep going. That's the last thing they would expect and anyway they don't even suspect anything. It's got to be our best chance. As soon as Nickolaus Kesling's parents see me it's all over.'

Ruth nodded in agreement, for a second or two they were both silent.

'I'm frightened Ernie.' He walked over and hugged her tight.

'Me too girl,' gently he kissed her forehead then looked in to her eyes, 'We've come this far,' she nodded her head positively and smiled. 'Whatever happens Ruth I want you to know,' he hesitated for a split second, 'I love you.' Her eyes started glistening with tears. 'Don't cry,' before she could reply there was a bang on the door,

'Rottenführer Kesling are you in there?' Two guards stood outside the toilet, 'The presentation is about to begin, could you please come immediately.' Ruth opened the door.

'One minute he will be out,'

'Thank you Fraulein.' She closed the door; the two guards looked at each other trying to control their laughter, they made suggestive gestures to each other as to what the war hero was getting up to in the toilets with his nurse.

'There are two of them and they are both armed,' whispered Ruth.

'Shit,' said Ernie. One he could have dealt with, but two and both armed; it wasn't going to happen.

'Listen,' said Ruth, 'I will try to keep hold of your arm. When I squeeze just like we did earlier nod and smile, worst comes to the worst, faint.'

'What?' said Ernie,

'Just do it, I will tell them you are not well and Ernie, I love you too.'

'Rottenführer Kesling, please sir, we have to go now,' came a shout from outside. They briefly kissed then Ruth opened the door.

Intrigued by Ernie's story, Alex was still firmly holding the Iron Cross. Absorbing every detail, he hadn't realised Ernie's storytelling was gathering quite an audience. A young man in his mid-teens and his father both appeared transfixed by the old man's tale. Even a couple of old ladies out for a mooch around the shops looked captivated.

Ernie, now oblivious to his task of relieving himself of seven boxes of poppies, didn't notice that already at least half were gone. Alex interrupted him.

'So you obviously went through with it then?' handing him back the Iron Cross. 'The presentation I mean.'

'Yes,' replied Ernie.

'But what about Kesling's parents? How did you get round that one?'

'I guess it was fate,' said Ernie with a smile. 'I think it was just a case of the right place at the right time, you see what happened was…'

Ernie and Ruth followed the two soldiers back towards the reception area, both praying they were not confronted by Kesling's overjoyed parents. The room was empty and outside the windows they could see a large crowd gathering. 'Please sir, this way, we have no time,' said one of the soldiers looking a little agitated. They followed them straight through another room and outside via large french doors.

The outside of the palace was as stunning as the interior, with its yellow stone walls and superbly sculptured figurines around the windows and roof. The grounds seem to go on forever with flights of stairs leading down to separate beautifully manicured gardens.

'Please, Rottenführer Kesling,' the soldier ushered Ernie onto the end of a rank of soldiers. Some showed the signs of battle, others stood bolt upright. Some twenty yards or so in front of them was the biggest gathering of high ranking officers Ernie had ever seen. They easily outnumbered the soldiers being honoured two to one. Ruth still held his arm, trying to stay as far to the rear as possible. Thirty or forty yards to the right, a large group of civilians, maybe as many as ten deep, stood behind a rope barrier. Every two or three steps an armed guard monitored every movement within the crowd. Suddenly an officer at the end of Ernie's line called out.

'Attention!' Even the injured did their best to stand up straight, Ernie included. From the door that Ernie had walked through not two minutes earlier came a group of men. The first two appeared to be scanning everyone and everything within close proximity. Then Ernie couldn't believe his eyes, he almost said, 'Oh my God,' but swallowed hard instead. Adolf Hitler and his entourage entered the room. Ruth unintentionally squeezed Ernie's arm, he thought about it for a second then just smiled, realising the action was more from fear than anything else. Hitler first walked along the line of officers, each saluting him as he went by. Occasionally he would stop and exchange a word or two, but never for more than a second. He stood in front of the line of soldiers to be decorated and began to give a speech. All Ernie picked up on was something about 'Sons of the Fatherland,' and 'We will never surrender,' or something along those lines. Ernie thought for a moment that he had heard that speech somewhere before. To rapturous applause, Hitler walked over to the line of soldiers. One by one, from the far end, he presented them with their medals. Finally, he reached Ernie, who could feel Ruth shaking on his arm.

'Congratulations, you are a true son and hero of the Fatherland.' Ruth squeezed his arm tight, Ernie smiled and bowed forward. It seemed to work, Hitler stepped back. The officer again called, 'Attention!' every soldier in the proximity adhered to the command. Hitler raised his arm in salute and walked back through the door into the palace, closely followed by his entourage and bodyguards.

A little further back in the crowd than they would have liked to have been, Nickolaus Kesling's parents strained their necks for a glimpse of their son. The debris on the road leaving Berlin had made them late; they almost missed the presentation completely. Nickolaus's father, Otto, could see the last three or four soldiers being honoured, but no sign of his son. For one reason or another, it had been over twelve months since he had any leave. So, not only was it a great honour to see the presentation, but they were anxious to spend as much time with him as possible.

Until their Führer was safely in his staff car, the guards kept everyone under tight control. There had been a number of attempts on his life, and it wasn't going to happen on their watch. Some of the newly decorated soldiers identified family in the crowd and waved in their direction to acknowledge them. The guards stood firm, following orders to the letter. Still the Keslings could not see their beloved son.

Ruth again squeezed Ernie's arm, he turned and she said, 'Toilet.' He nodded and they walked back into the palace through the door they had come through. An officer called out to the guards to let the families through to their loved ones, and a surge of people came forward; some quickly found their sons, others took a little longer. The Keslings kept looking. Where was he? They had been told he was definitely here.

'Don't worry dear we'll find him,' said Otto Kesling to his wife. He also had been a hero of the Fatherland, gassed in the trenches during the First World War. He would have gladly gone with his son into the army, but his age and health were against him. Finally he was refused on medical grounds.

Otto went over to the officer who had called the soldiers to attention. His name was Karl Fleischer. At six feet six with the straightest back humanly possible, he was a staunch Nazi. Exactly what Hitler visualised as his German super race.

'Excuse me, my name is Otto Kesling, my son was decorated here today and I don't seem to be able to find him.'

'Good afternoon Herr Kesling,' said the officer, looking down. 'He is definitely here I saw the Reich Führer present him with the Iron Cross with my own eyes, you must be very proud.'

'That I am sir, but where has he gone?' The officer's height enabled him when standing on his tip toes to see right across the crowd.

'Hmm, he was stood right at the end, the last man on the line. He had two sticks so he can't have gone far.'

Otto raised his hand and gently rubbed his forehead with his index finger and thumb, a method he used to retrieve his thoughts. In his mind he went over the presentation, he hadn't got the best view but he could see the last few soldiers. Closing his eyes he remembered the soldier at the end. Yes he thought, he had two sticks, looked very unsteady on his feet had a nurse with him; that's what brought his attention to him. But it wasn't his son, definitely not his son.

'That was not my son,' said Otto. His wife came over.

'Any luck Otto?'

'Good afternoon Frau Kesling,' said Fleischer, 'there seems to be a little confusion with the whereabouts of your son. He seems to have wandered off.'

'He hasn't wandered off,' said Otto becoming irritated, 'I'm beginning to wonder if he was here at all.'

'Please, please Herr Kesling, I will get my men to find him. Stay calm and I will sort it out.' With that Fleischer strode off in the direction of a group of guards.

Ernie and Ruth were already by the entrance to the palace, which was still swarming with soldiers. They thought about taking a staff car, but they wouldn't even get through the road block. The car they arrived in was gone. They had probably intended for him to stay with his parents while he was recovering. What they had intended for Ruth, he hadn't a clue. Best thing they could do was lay low until the security level was reduced within the town and palace. Now moving very quickly on his sticks, Ruth was almost running to keep up. Looking up, under his breath Ernie said, 'See the old windmill?' Ruth nodded. 'If we can get in we might be able to lay low there, come on.' Following a path around the inside edge of the palace wall, they climbed to the mill. Its condition looked worse the closer they got, but that might just be a godsend. It might just be that it had been locked up to the public until it could be properly renovated. Looking down towards the entrance they could see soldiers clearing away sandbags and dismantling roadblocks. If they could just evade capture until after dark, nine out of ten soldiers would be back to their usual duties and they might just be able to slip away unnoticed. The stone base of the windmill was intact. Up above was a wooden balcony. Parts of it looked damaged but the majority was intact. That alone was enough to keep the public out. Being very careful not to be seen, they walked around the perimeter. There was a wooden door with a latch-type fastening, no sign of any chains or locks. Ernie tried the door. Surprisingly, it opened. Cautiously they both went in, closing the door behind them.

It didn't look as if there had been much activity in there for a while. Leaning against the walls were a few gardening tools and some tools Ernie hadn't a clue about. Continuing to scan around the mill they saw a narrow staircase leading up to another floor. Ernie went first. They climbed the stairs, trying to be as quiet as possible. He peeked his head up onto the next floor; it looked deserted. There were a few piles of old sacks, a small table and two chairs. Hanging on a line of hooks on the wall were what looked like old overalls, and neatly placed below, two pairs of boots.

It didn't look particularly dusty so someone must have been there recently. Another small staircase led to the third and final floor. Feeling quite sure there was nobody there, they climbed up the final staircase. The room was very narrow, verging on claustrophobic, but hopefully a safe haven for at least a few hours. Like the lower floor it was sparsely furnished with nothing more than a rickety chair, a few old tea chests and another big pile of sacks. Ernie laid out all the sacks in as comfortable position possible and lay down with his back propped up against one of the tea chests. Ruth got down and cuddled up beside him. He put his arm round her shoulder and held her tight. Returning the gesture she put her arm across his waist and squeezed.

'It's going to be alright isn't it Ernie?' He kissed the top of her head.

'No problem,' replied Ernie trying to reassure her, 'cakewalk.' His mind flashed back to a few months earlier when a young man had said just the same thing. They both lay in silence with their thoughts, hoping their disappearance had not been discovered.

'So what happened to the Keslings, they must have been beside themselves with worry?' said Alex, now perching precariously on the edge of his seat. Suddenly, from the rear of the small audience, a man asked, 'But how did you get away in that SS uniform- you would have stood out like a sore thumb?' The rest of Ernie's audience turned and looked at him. Realising he was eavesdropping, he raised his eyebrows and shoulders, feeling slightly embarrassed. Very sheepishly he said, 'Sorry.'

'I was just getting to that, you see what happened was...'

The Keslings were now incensed with the situation that had unfolded. The guards had come back with no sign of the war hero or his nurse.

'Herr and Frau Kesling,' said Fleischer, 'I am doing everything in my power to locate your son.' Hearing the officer call the man in the line his son was like a red rag to a bull.

'For the last time,' said Otto Kesling raising his voice, 'that was not my son. Who is your superior officer? I want to see him now.' The heated exchange was starting to attract a lot of attention. From the gathering of high ranking officers, one in particular, a General Burgdorf, thought he would intervene. As he approached the Keslings, Fleischer suddenly stopped talking and came to attention.

'Good day, I am General Burgdorf. Does there seem to be a problem?'

Looking very flustered, Otto Kesling said, 'Good day General, it appears my son Nickolaus Kesling has disappeared, but as I have been saying for the last half an hour, the man who received his commendation was not my son. He's an impostor.'

Hearing the accusation, the general suggested they go inside and sort it out. The Keslings now felt relieved and pleased that someone was taking their accusation seriously. Initially General Burgdorf just wanted to move the couple from the main gathering, as they were lowering the tone of the proceedings. But once he heard the whole story, his attitude changed. He sent one of the guards to get Fleischer, as he had been dealing with the Kesling's crisis. The officer strode into the room, as usual, bolt upright. The general was sat at a table facing the Keslings. He walked up to the general and came to attention.

'You called for me sir.' The general stood up, rubbing his chin and looking very thoughtful he said, 'Hauptmann (Captain) Fleischer, how many men did you send to locate Rottenführer Kesling?'

'Four sir.'

The general took a large breath and slowly walked around the room, 'And where did they search?'

'Everywhere, sir,' Fleischer hesitated, 'well, everywhere within the palace.'

The general licked his lips and again took a very large breath, 'so they never went into the hundreds of acres of grounds or asked at the main gate if he had left.'

'No sir, I didn't think...' he never got to finish his sentence. The general's tone of voice raised by about fifty decibels,

'WELL MAYBE IF YOU HAD WE WOULDN'T BE IN THIS SITUATION.' The officer was now standing bolt upright,

'Yes sir.' Even the Keslings felt themselves sitting up straight in their chairs. Calming his voice, the general stood behind Fleischer and leaned close to his shoulder. 'I want you to go to the main entrance and ask if the man in question was seen leaving the palace. He can't be hard to spot he could barely walk and had a nurse with him. Then I want you to get every available man and search every part of the palace till you find him.'

'But sir, there are over six hundred acres of grounds.' The general took another deep breath and swallowed, as if he was trying to calm himself down.

'I will remind you again, we are looking for a man on sticks with a nurse, how far do you think he would have got?' Feeling a little silly the officer bowed his head and said,

'I will deal with it immediately sir.'

A little condescendingly the general replied, 'Thank you.' Again Fleischer stood up straight and delivered the Nazi salute. 'Heil Hitler,' turned to the Keslings, clicked his heals and bowed. He about turned and left the room red faced.

'Right then,' said the general smiling broadly, 'can I interest you both in a drink? I would love to hear about your son. Rottenführer Kesling has become a hero not only to the German public but also within the ranks.' With that he escorted them both back to the gathering, attempting to keep the peace with charm and champagne.

Most of the soldiers Fleischer spoke to on the gate had either recently been assigned to the position or hadn't seen anyone of that description. Not wanting to incur the wrath of General Burgdorf he rounded up thirty men, briefed them on the situation and sent them in pairs with orders to search anywhere and everywhere. The man in question must be found.

Ruth had fallen asleep and was lying with her head on Ernie's stomach. Always the soldier, Ernie stayed vigilant, his arm firmly holding onto Ruth's waist. Old buildings make a lot of noise, and this one was no exception. It was starting to get dark. He wasn't sure what the time was, but at this time of the year the nights were cold and they were long. Suddenly, his senses where alerted to the sound of a door opening. As far as he knew there was only one way in and one way out of the mill. Gently, he shook Ruth's shoulder. As she woke and looked up at him he raised a finger to his mouth telling her not to make a sound.

On the ground floor a man by the name of Hendrick Bauer had entered the mill. Already a retired citizen, he worked in the palace grounds voluntarily. He had lived in Potsdam all his life. Now at 67 years of age, he loved tending to the lawns and flowers. In the winter he was engaged in the general upkeep of the grounds. It kept him fit and gave him a reason to get out of bed in the morning. He always kept his personal gardening tools in the mill; whenever he left them out they would disappear for days on end. He placed his fork and shovel against the wall. Looking down at his boots, they were caked in soil.

'If you go home with feet like that she'll give your ears a bending,' he said to himself. He slowly dropped to one knee, grimacing as his weight put pressure on his ageing joints. Slowly he struggled to pick a knot out of his lace and slipped his boot off, then repeated with the other foot. Ernie got up and almost silently went to the top of the stairs and peered down; suddenly he heard footsteps on the ground floor stairs, it sounded like somebody mumbling to themselves. Ernie tiptoed back to the sacks, his intention to get as many sacks on top of them as possible and just hope they wouldn't be discovered. There was a cracking sound and one of the floor boards gave way under Ernie's foot. The gardener still mumbling to himself stopped in his tracks. He wasn't quite on the second floor but straightaway his senses told him he wasn't alone.

'Hello,' he shouted, expecting an instant reply, nothing came. Ernie looked at Ruth and pointed at the sacks, gesturing with his hands to hide. Again the gardener shouted, 'Hello up there,' still no reply. Slowly, and with great caution, he climbed up to the second floor. He looked around the room; his spare boots were where he left them under his overalls. He walked over to them and slid his feet in, leaving the laces undone. He peered up the last flight of stairs, and at the top of his voice he shouted, 'Is there anyone up there?' Still no reply. He started to doubt himself. Did he really hear a floorboard give way or was it just the old timbers in the mill creaking like everything else in this palace, tired with age?

His curiosity was getting the better of him, he had to look. He started to climb the stairs; he could feel his hands trembling. 'Silly old man it's probably just rats,' he said to himself. Finding a little Dutch courage he climbed the last few steps more rapidly. As he looked over the top into the room it all looked fine, just as he had left it a few days earlier. Except the sacks. His eyes widened as he saw a boot and it moved very slightly, but it moved. 'Come out, I know you're under there.'

Ruth and Ernie knew they had been discovered. Their hearts dropped, expecting to be confronted by a German soldier yielding a machine gun, or worse still, more than one. Ernie threw back the sacks and both men stared into each other's eyes, neither seeing what they expected. The gardener, seeing Ernie's uniform and then Ruth, thought it was a soldier trying to have a bit of privacy with his sweetheart. Ernie and Ruth both breathed a sigh of relief that there wasn't a gun pointing at them. Both parties were lost for words, and Ruth said,

'Good evening sir.' The gardener was about to apologise for interrupting them when he noticed Ernie's sticks leaning against the wall. Slowly he put two and two together. He had been asked by three or four soldiers that afternoon if he had seen an SS soldier on sticks accompanied by a nurse. Of course he hadn't, but if he did he must report them immediately, it was of grave importance they were found. He raised his hand,

'You're the ones they're looking for, I have to report you.' He started backing down the stairs, his eyes firmly fixed on Ernie's. Ruth turned to Ernie. In English she said, 'He knows who we are.' Ernie got to his feet, he couldn't let him get away. The old man was already down the first flight of stairs. Ernie followed as quickly as he could.

'Wait,' shouted Ernie, the old man stopped, shocked to hear him speaking in English. 'I don't want to hurt you, but I can't let you go.' Ruth by now was right behind Ernie and she repeated what he said in German. The old man was visibly shaken. Each step he took backwards, Ernie moved forward, slowly closing the distance between them.

Clumsily with his eyes still firmly fixed on Ernie's, his toes and heels searched for the top stair.

Ernie put his hand out, 'Wait.' Suddenly the old man's legs buckled as his one foot missed the step completely. As he fell backwards Ernie lunged forwards in an attempt to grab the old man and prevent him from falling. It was no good; the back of the old man's head careered into a large timber beam, a gaping wound opened on the base of his skull, blood splattered across the beam as he fell. The gardner snatched at anything and everything in an attempt to prevent the inevitable, but it was in vain. He landed on the back of his neck with a sickening crack. Death was instantaneous; his contorted body lay motionless at the bottom of the stairs. Ruth covered her face with her hands as she gasped with shock. Ernie quickly dashed down the stairs in the hope he could help the old man. As Ernie felt his neck for a pulse, the gardner's lifeless eyes stared up towards Ruth, tears now running down her face.

Ernie went very quiet.

'You OK Ernie?' asked Alex concerned by the old man's anguished expression.

Ernie took a deep breath, and after a long pause he said, 'I have seen a lot of men killed and maimed, but that man's death has haunted me to this day. He didn't deserve to finish his life that way.'

Alex interrupted him, 'You could say the same for so many people during war. Unfortunately the innocent sometimes get caught up in the madness of it all, and anyway if he hadn't fallen you might not be here now.'

'The old man must have been missed, so what did you do then?' called out a young man within the group listening to Ernie's story.

Ernie looked up at him, 'Well it turned out to be a touch of luck for us; you see I finally managed to get out of that SS uniform.'

Ruth came down the stairs. 'He's dead,' said Ernie. Ruth looked scared stiff, her face very pale. Ernie had seen it before in young soldiers experiencing battle for the first time.

'What are we going to do?' asked Ruth, visibly shaking.

Ernie stood up, 'Come here,' Ruth quickly found the comfort of Ernie's arm's. Holding her tight he said, 'Don't worry, he can't hurt us now and we haven't been discovered.' Slowly Ruth calmed down. Ernie knew time wasn't on their side, they had to act and quickly.

'Listen, I have to get out of this uniform, he's only slightly bigger than me,' Ruth didn't speak, just nodded. 'You get his boots off.'

Swiftly Ernie stripped out of his uniform, Ruth did as he asked. Once changed, they stowed the old man's body behind the staircase. Ernie went back up the stairs and threw down a large pile of sacks. Once they had covered the body Ernie took his uniform upstairs and hid it. The further it was from the old man's body the better. Hopefully when discovered, they wouldn't put two and two together, at least not straight away.

It was dark and getting very cold. The Keslings, both extremely upset, had been sent home a few hours earlier. General Burgdorf had promised them he would personally deal with the situation and keep them informed of his progress. Assuming the couple had left the palace, the search was to be extended to the surrounding town and countryside. If the truth was known, it wasn't high on General Burgdorf's agenda. At the same time in the back of his mind, he thought, 'If the man was an imposter...who knows? Maybe an assassin; look how close he had got to their beloved Führer.'

For this reason alone he had to get to the bottom of it. He sent a messenger to contact an old friend of his, a man by the name of Herman Kohl, not well-known in the military, but known well-enough to captured spies and informers, especially around Paris during the occupation of the city. A ruthless individual, the only words to describe him would be a sick sadist. The message asked for him to come to the Sanssouci Palace that evening. He had a task of the utmost urgency.

Ernie and Ruth wrapped up as warmly as the clothing they had allowed. They both decided it was time to make a break for it under the cover of darkness. Whichever way they went it was going to be dangerous. They knew the main road was guarded or at least it had been earlier that afternoon so their best bet was to head across the palace grounds, and once out of the grounds, to just keep going west trying to avoid built-up areas. Ernie slowly opened the mill door, instantly feeling the drop in temperature. It was bitterly cold, but they had to get away. Peering into the darkness he listened, straining his ears for the slightest noise.

Once satisfied there was no one about, he gestured to Ruth to follow him. Surprisingly, it was very quiet; in fact, there wasn't a soul about. After scurrying down a grass embankment they stopped behind a large hedge. Their position offered a good view of the rear of the palace. There were very dim lights, probably the glow from strategically placed candles, unusual at this time of night due to the severity of the bombing on Berlin; possibly to enable the staff to continue with their work. The occasional figure walked past a window but thankfully no sign of soldiers. Keeping low they made their way along the hedgerow till they were a good 150 metres away from the palace.

The vines and hedges at this distance completely hid them from any staff or guards that might still be patrolling the back of the palace. The grounds were vast and vine after vine, seemed to go on forever. They passed a large circular pool. At a glance there appeared to be a large ornate sculpture in the middle, probably a fountain; they veered off left, trying to keep from the main path. Pausing for a moment they looked back at the outline of the palace. In peaceful times it must have been an incredible sight, all lit up, fountains and palace. Unfortunately, not that night. With the constant threat of Allied bombers dispatching their payload upon Berlin, it was inevitable that beautiful historic landmarks, such as this one, would be dragged into the turmoil of war.

After a good 30 minutes they came to a wall with iron railings above. It had to be the perimeter wall. In the darkness they couldn't see a gate or entrance of any kind. The wall was high, but even with his injured leg, not a problem. Jumping up and grabbing the railings he scampered his feet on the wall till he was standing. Quickly he dropped to a crouching position, the pain in his leg causing him to grimace. From this vantage point he had a good look around; it looked all clear. He reached down with one hand, offering Ruth a means to climb, his other hand stayed firmly fixed on the railings.

'Ready?' asked Ernie, Ruth nodded and leapt at the wall. Ernie pulled with all his might, 'Grab the bars girl.' Ruth did as he said and after a short scramble was on the wall crouched alongside him. The railings were arched with ornate spikes initially fitted as a means of fortification. The last thing they needed now was to get an arm or leg impaled. Ernie edged his way to the lowest part of the arch. 'Be careful Ruth, I'll go first.' With both hands holding the top of the bars Ernie leapt up easily lifting his own body weight over the top. Relying on crutches for the last few months had strengthened his already wiry strong upper body. Once stood on the other side it was Ruth's turn. She jumped up, but the strength required to lift her own body weight over the railings was too much for her. It was no good, she fell back to her feet on top of the wall. 'Come on girl you can do it,' said Ernie enthusiastically, she tried again, this time using her feet to scramble up the bars. Again she held the position for a few seconds, and then fell back to her feet.

'It's no good, I'm just not strong enough.'

Ernie thought for a moment, there had to be a way. 'Right, I have an idea,' Ernie got down on his knees, precariously balancing on top of the wall. He put his hands through the bars, one on top of the other with his palms facing up. 'Right, I want you to step on my hands, when I say jump give it everything you've got, I'll lift you as high as I can.' Ruth determinedly bit her lip and nodded her head.

'Ready?' Ruth took a deep breath. 'Jump.' Ernie pulled up with all his might and Ruth went so high her hands left the bars. Ernie had visions of her coming down and impaling her hand or worse still, her stomach on the spikes. Thankfully she missed them. Ernie endeavoured to hold her weight above the spikes, 'Right, cock your leg over,' she did as he said, placing her shin on his shoulder, 'and the other one.' As her weight transferred over the railings, he lowered her down his body onto the top of the wall. She squeezed him tight and he could feel her heart pounding. Attempting to calm her down he returned the gesture.

'There you go, piece of cake,' his words belying how fast his own heart was pounding. They jumped down onto a grass verge. In front of them was a narrow road, then open fields. 'Shall we?' asked Ernie, Ruth nodded. Staying low, looking both ways, they raced across the road and into the fields, as fast as their legs would carry them, quickly disappearing into the night.

Unknown to Ernie and Ruth, virtually at the same time they made their escape from the palace grounds, General Burgdorf sat in a relaxing armchair silently spinning a large glass of brandy. He was awaiting the arrival of his old friend Herman Kohl. Opposite him, bolt upright and looking very uncomfortable, Hauptmann Fleischer sat on the edge of a dining room chair, not really sure why and what the general had in store for him. All he knew was the man who was shortly to join them had a reputation, and not a pleasant one. The silence was starting to get to Fleischer, when suddenly a knock on the door broke the uneasy atmosphere.

'Enter,' called out the general, a guard opened the door and stepped just inside.

'Herr Kohl has arrived sir, would you like me to show...' the guard did not finish. As rudely as humanly possible the guard was pushed out of the doorway. The kafuffle caused Fleischer to jump to his feet, but the general just gave a knowing grin. Stood in the doorway was Herman Kohl, Fleischer couldn't believe his eyes. All the things he had heard about this tyrant: and there in front of him was an ageing, overweight, five foot seven balding man, with a long black leather coat that made him look shorter than he actually was. Fleischer realised his mouth was open; quickly he closed it and stood straight. At his height Kohl was virtually a midget.

'Herr General,' said Kohl with his arms wide open. The guard, annoyed by the man's arrogance, gritted his teeth but remembered his place and backed off, closing the door as he left the room.

The general got up out of his chair, his expression that of a man who had just been reunited with his brother after a long absence.

'Herman,' walking over to each other, they embraced, 'it's been too long. You're looking well my old friend.' Fleischer thought, if this is looking well, what the hell was he like before? The general turned to Fleischer. 'Herman, I would like to introduce you to Hauptmann

Fleischer.' Fleischer put his boots together and bowed forward, then raised his arm.

'Heil Hitler.'

'Heil Hitler,' Kohl replied, straining his neck looking up at him. 'Your reputation precedes you sir,' said Fleischer,

'All good I hope, Hauptmann Fleischer?'

'Of course sir.'

'Ummm,' murmured Kohl, a little sceptical of Fleischer's statement.

'Please gentlemen, have a seat.' interrupted the general. I would like to get straight down to the reason for our meeting, as time is of the utmost urgency.' The general and Kohl moved across the room to a table. Fleischer picked up the dining chair he had been sitting on and joined them. The general put the tips of his fingers together. Looking at his hands, he tapped his thumbs together thinking about the best way to approach the conversation.

'This afternoon our beloved Führer presented a number of soldiers with commendations. One in particular, a Nickolaus Kesling, you may have heard a little about him, there was a big propaganda drive on him after a battle outside of Arnhem a few months ago.' Fleischer and Kohl looked puzzled. 'Anyway that's not important now. His parents arrived to see the ceremony. Afterwards they clearly identified the man as an imposter. Low and behold, he and his nurse haven't been seen since the allegation was made. The man could hardly walk, but the palace and grounds, plus part of the local area, have been searched. We can't find him. What worried me was how close he got to the Führer. I want you to track him down, I'm not concerned about the nurse but I want that man. I promised his parents I would get to the bottom of it, and I don't make promises lightly.'

Kohl's head slowly moved up and down as licked his lips then he said, 'We have to assume the sticks could have been a decoy, just to make us assume he can't get far. What resources are available to me, sorry, us?' glancing at Fleischer.

'I can give you twenty men plus vehicles,' said the general, 'but please gentlemen, I need a conclusion on this.' The general looked directly at Kohl. 'Herman, I wouldn't have asked if it wasn't important, you know that.'

Kohl pushed his chair back and stood up, 'Consider it done my friend, have your men ready to move in one hour.'

A smile appeared on the general's face, 'That's what I wanted to hear my friend.'

Fleischer stood up, towering above Kohl, 'I will rally the men.'

'Good,' said Kohl. 'I would like to spend another hour before we leave just checking outbuildings close to the palace, if the sticks were really needed they will be holed-up close by.'

Fleischer agreed.

'Good hunting,' said the general. Both men respectfully bowed their heads. Fleischer, as always, gave the Nazi salute, tapping the heels of his boots together. Kohl felt obliged and responded. With that they left the meeting. Burgdorf stood up and slowly walked over to the window. Still spinning his glass of brandy he looked into the darkness and said, 'Where are you?'

Ironically, had he had stood in the same place not thirty minutes earlier, from their vantage point in the darkness, Ernie and Ruth would have seen him in the window.

The crowd around Ernie fluctuated; every now and then another member of the public would gather around trying to see what the attraction was. Then another would respectfully move on, their Sunday lunch taking priority over an old man's memories. Not Alex. Hearing Ernie's story right from the beginning and combined with his military background meant he was still transfixed.

'It must have been freezing Ernie,' said Alex, 'you being a hardened soldier in those days, I can see you handling it, but Ruth? How did she cope? I mean you had no real warm clothing to speak off and no food.' Ernie shook his head.

'I don't mind saying I was worried, of course I never told Ruth that. I was colder than I can ever remember but we had no choice, we just had to keep going.'

They walked long into the night. Assuming the old gardener would be missed by the morning they had to put as much distance between themselves and the palace as possible. They decided the best plan would be to walk by night under cover of darkness, and find somewhere to rest up in the day. Even with his injured leg Ernie set a pace Ruth struggled to maintain. Stopping to rest was out of the question. Seeing the tiredness and pain in Ruth's face was killing him inside, but if they were going to get through this, he had to put his emotional feelings behind him, for now at least. The temperature had dropped even further. If they stopped, as tired as they were, falling asleep could be the end of them.

Far in the distance the signs of dawn began to show through the night sky and along with it came an even greater chill. It was time to look for somewhere to rest and hopefully some form of nourishment; but under the circumstances nourishment would be a luxury. As the darkness began to lift, some way off to their left the silhouette of what appeared to be farm outbuildings loomed on the horizon. Glancing at each other words weren't necessary. The two changed course and headed straight for them. Ruth was beginning to struggle, every step was a challenge, the cold and sheer exhaustion of the night's walk was taking its toll.

As they approached, Ernie told Ruth to wait while he checked out the buildings, but Ruth's face said it all: waiting around wasn't an option.

With a hint of a smile Ernie said, 'We'll go together, but stay behind me.' With her body now shaking uncontrollably Ruth rubbed her hands together and just nodded. As they got close they crouched down and took a moment to observe the buildings, looking for any sign of movement. Being as quiet as possible they moved in and edged their way around the perimeter of the buildings, looking for any open door or window they could access. All the buildings looked as if they had seen better days, but not enough to suspect they were derelict or uninhabited.

Ernie found what appeared to be a stable, the top half of the door was slightly ajar. He gently pushed it and without a sound it swung open. Ernie looked into the darkness as he reached over and felt for a bolt on the lower half of the door. Suddenly the sound of movement inside made him recoil back from the entrance. He looked at Ruth and raised a finger to his lips. Again he peered over the top of the door, straining his eyes to see what was there. With much relief he saw cows; four in all, huddled together in the corner surrounded by bales of hay. Not wanting to startle them he slowly opened the door. Ruth followed him in and closed the doors behind them. Instantly noticing a rise in the temperature Ernie rubbed his hands together. The animals didn't seem in any way concerned by their presence, just like Ernie and Ruth, staying warm was their main concern. The cows were all sat down side by side, just leaving enough space for them to clamber into the corner. Once in, they gathered as much hay around them as possible. The smell was unpleasant but a small sacrifice for their now warm corner of the building. Ernie put his arms around Ruth and squeezed her tight as he rubbed her shoulders.

'Let's get some sleep and see what the morning brings,' said Ernie as he kissed the top of her head. Ruth put her arms around his waist and held him tight. Barely able to keep her eyes open she quickly drifted off into a deep sleep.

Ernie tried to stay awake, at least for a little while just in case they had been seen entering the building. Ernie felt more protective of her than anyone he had ever known. In the few months they had been together, they had faced more danger than most couples would face in a lifetime. As her grip around his waist loosened, he also felt himself drifting off to sleep. Soon they both lay sideways in the hay, still holding on to each other, physically and mentally exhausted, oblivious to the world around them.

A few hours earlier the search of the palace outbuildings had continued in haste. The general knew that with Herman Kohl on-board he would get a result one way or another. Hauptmann Fleischer didn't like the idea of working with Kohl. Fleischer, being a staunch military man, believed that the Gestapo were nothing more than jumped-up bully boys with authority, but orders were orders.

It didn't take long to find the old gardener's body, and it was more by luck than judgement. With the exception of an old shed the windmill was the first building they searched. The guards sent news to Kohl and Fleischer who quickly arrived. Further investigation of the mill revealed Ernie's SS uniform and sticks.

They immediately reported back to General Burgdorf, it was obvious after putting two and two together they had an imposter. The general was furious, he freed up another ten men to help hunt them down. He wasn't concerned so much about the woman, but this man had the audacity to receive another man's commendation and make a mockery of their beloved Führer. Raising his voice, something Kohl had never seen him do, he told them he wanted this man kneeling at his feet within twenty-four hours. Kohl assured him he would make it happen. In the early hours of the morning, a staff car and a canvas topped truck loaded with soldiers rolled out of the Sanssouci Palace, their sole purpose to hunt down Ernie and Ruth.

With the sunrise came the familiar sound of a cockerel crowing. Ernie and Ruth slept soundly, oblivious to the figure stood in the stable door way. With a stick in his right hand, he stepped forward and tapped the cows one by one on their haunches. The cows immediately got up and one by one filed out into the yard, apparently an everyday occurrence. He prodded Ernie with the point of his stick. Ernie, still exhausted stirred but didn't wake up. The man took a deep breath sighed and shook his head all in one. He walked back to the door and banged his stick loudly on the side of the frame. Ernie and Ruth woke with a jolt, startled and fearing the worst.

'It's a lot warmer in the farm house and you're welcome to some food and drink before you go, take it or leave it.' said the farmer. With that he turned and walked off. Not being able to understand him, Ernie wasn't sure if he was talking to them or somebody outside the door. They both sat up.

'What did he say?' asked Ernie looking at Ruth.

'He offered us food and drink,' said Ruth, still looking extremely tired. 'Sooner or later we have to eat Ernie, just let me do all the talking.

I'll tell him you can't talk due to your neck injury.' Ernie agreed, they both got up and brushed down their clothes, Ruth used the palms of her hands in an attempt to make her hair look presentable.

'Ready?' asked Ernie offering her his hand.

'As I'll ever be,' came the reply. Hand in hand they walked out into the yard, where they saw the farmer disappear into what must have been the farmhouse.

Cautiously they went over. Ruth went first, closely followed by Ernie. As they stepped onto the porch they noticed the door was slightly ajar, left for them to enter. Like timid animals being offered food they edged forward through the door. It was a very run-down but functional country style kitchen. In the centre of the room a table surrounded by four chairs had been set for a meal. Stood by the sink an elderly woman washed up the remainder of some pots from a previous meal. She appeared completely oblivious to Ernie and Ruth's presence.

'Sit yourselves down, breakfast will be ready shortly,' came a voice from the next room. Ruth looked at Ernie and gestured for him to sit. Choosing the seats with backs to the door they both sat. In the middle of the table there was a large crusty loaf, some butter, and a large chunk of cheese. Unknowingly they were both staring at the food. Both their stomachs growled with hunger, but respectfully they waited to be offered. From the doorway of the next room a farmer appeared, his stature was that of a younger man, but his pure white hair and the lines on his face indicated he had experienced many hard winters.

'We don't want to know your business; there are a lot of people on the road looking for friends and family, others just trying to escape the madness of this war.'

'Thank you,' said Ruth, 'it's very kind of you to take us in like this.'

'We're not taking you in.'

Ruth jumped in, 'I'm sorry I didn't mean to...'

He interrupted her.

'Just have a good meal, rest a little then be on your way.'

The woman at the sink just carried on washing pots, not in the slightest bit interested in who they were or why they had spent a night in the stable. From the oven they smelt an aroma they hadn't smelled for some time, bacon, it smelt wonderful.

'Help yourself to bread and cheese; we have the last of our bacon in the oven. You're welcome to share some with us once it's cooked.'

'We really do appreciate this,' said Ruth picking up the bread knife. The farmer went over to the window sill and picked up a large jug of milk.

He placed it on the table followed by two glasses. Then he walked over to the sink, held the woman's arm and she stopped what she was doing.

'Come on dear, sit yourself down,' he said in a gentle voice. She did not speak, just shuffled round on her feet, and with her eyes staring straight ahead she felt for his arm. Once she had a secure grip on his forearm she walked forward towards the table. Straight away they realised she was blind, or visually impaired. Her eyes looked misty, probably cataracts on both eyes that had become progressively worse over a long period of time. Still holding tight on his forearm with one hand, she felt for the back of the chair.

Once she was sat down, still staring ahead she reached out across the table for Ruth's hand. Ruth realised what she was trying to do and offered it to her. The old lady held it in both hands like a palmist searching for information from every line and callous. After a few seconds she said,

'You have never worked the land, but I feel a friendly warmth in you, even though your hands are cold.'

'Thank you,' said Ruth, 'we walked all night it was very cold.' Raising her eyes towards Ruth's, sensing rather than seeing she asked, 'Where do you come from?'

'My parents lived in Berlin, but I don't know what happened to them.'

'That's not what I asked you.' It was strange but Ruth felt as if the old woman knew she was a Jew. How and why she couldn't explain, it was almost as if the woman had a sixth sense.

Comfortingly she tapped the back of Ruth's hand, 'This war has brought much sorrow and hardship.' Her tone suddenly changed, 'Curse them,' she said out loud spitting through her teeth. 'They took my boys you know,' she squeezed Ruth's hand, 'not a word, two years and not a word.'

The old woman squeezed hard, Ernie could see by Ruth's face she was in pain, he was just about to intervene when the farmer reached down and took hold of the woman's fingers, 'Calm down dear,' one by one he peeled them off to Ruth's relief. 'Can I apologise for my wife, she hasn't been well,' he held her shoulders gently and caringly. 'Come on dear, I think you need a little lie down.' A single tear rolled down her cheek.

'I am sorry,' she said.

'It's alright,' replied Ruth feeling the pain and anguish in the woman's voice. With her husband still holding her shoulders she stood up and slowly shuffled out of the room. Ruth looked at Ernie; he could see she was distressed.

'What was all that about?' he whispered. Ruth shook her head.

'The war I guess.' She picked up the knife and cut them both a generous slice of bread followed by cheese.

As Ernie and Ruth tucked into the food the farmer returned. 'You will have to excuse my wife.' Ernie paid little attention to his words and continued eating, his eyes fixed firmly on the meal.

'We understand,' said Ruth, 'this war has affected people in many ways.'

He looked at Ernie, 'Doesn't say a lot does he?' Ruth pointed at her own neck, 'He got shot in the neck, hasn't been able to speak since.'

Sarcastically he replied, 'Did it affect his ears as well?'

Ruth quickly latched on to what he meant and briskly nudged Ernie, pointing at her own neck she said in German, 'I was just saying about the injury to your neck.'

Ernie stopped eating for a moment and looked at her, half picking up what she meant by the hand gesture, he grimaced and held his hand to his own neck.

Trying to take the emphasis off Ernie, Ruth turned her attention back to the farmer, looking puzzled she said, 'Your wife mentioned something about her boys being taken away.'

He sat down on the chair facing them with his elbows on the table and rubbed his face with both hands. After a few seconds he said, 'Like nearly all the young men in this country they went as soon as they heard the call. I love my country,' again he hesitated, 'but these men in power,' he took a deep breath, 'last thing we heard they had gone to the Eastern front, Stalingrad, I have a picture of them both just before they went.' He stood up and went over to a dresser on which were half a dozen photographs. Picking one up, he returned to the table, proudly looking at the image of two young men and his wife. 'These are our boys,' he passed it to Ruth. 'Klaus is the tall one, the other is Gunter, both fine boys, I hoped they would take over the farm after the war, but now...' he paused.

Ruth and Ernie looked at the picture, they were both in uniform, their mother was stood between them looking very proud.

'They look very handsome fine young men.'

'That was the last day we saw them. At first the letters were regular and cheerful,' he looked down at the table, 'but then, I could tell things weren't right after the first winter, then the letters just stopped. She's been the same ever since. Her eyesight just compounded the problem.'

'We're very sorry,' said Ruth feeling the pain in his heart.

He pushed the chair away and stood up, 'What the hell, it's the war that should be sorry, not you.'

He turned and walked over to the oven, and, as he opened the door the aroma of cooked bacon went to another level. He slid out a tray with a good size bacon joint on it, the skin beautifully crisp. As he placed it on the table their eyes were transfixed on it. Not aware of their actions, they both licked their lips in anticipation of a slice or two. He picked up a large knife, 'Well, it's the last we have but you're welcome to share some with us.' Ruth's smile was gratitude enough. He began carving the meat.

'The smell of bacon, wonderful,' said Alex.

Ernie nodded his head, 'Every time I smell bacon I think of that moment, apart from the veg they had grown, that was all they had left, but they were still happy to share it with complete strangers.' Ernie shuffled in his chair trying to get a little more comfortable. 'Human nature never ceases to amaze me, I think he knew I wasn't German, but he still let me sit at his table and share his last meal.'

'How long did you stay?'

'Not long, after a good meal we didn't want to outstay our welcome. Any case, whether we wanted to stay or not wasn't up to us,'

'Why, did he ask you to leave?'

'No, nothing like that, the German military decided that.

They both sat back in their chairs.

'Thank you,' said Ruth, 'it's been a while since we have eaten so well.' The farmer took the remainder of the bacon, placed it on a large chopping board then covered it with a cloth. 'We have sat at your table and eaten your food, and we don't even know your name.'

'It doesn't matter,' replied the farmer. Ruth could feel the hurt in his voice.

'It does, you're a kind man, we won't forget you.' Her words started to get to him, he stood silently for a moment then said,

'Gerhard, my name is Gerhard Meyer and my wife's name is Edith.'

As he turned Ruth smiled, 'We are very pleased to meet you Gerhard.' He almost smiled sensing the people he had just given his last meal to were good people. The moment was suddenly broken by the distant sound of a truck engine over revving. Ernie jumped to his feet and dashed over to the window.

In English he said, 'Soldiers.'

The farmer didn't look surprised; he had already worked out Ernie was not German. Ruth instantly jumped up from her chair. They both looked at the farmer, without his help they were done for. His expression was that of, I don't need this trouble. A moment's hesitation and he said,

'Quickly, go out through the back yard. Keep low till you're behind the out buildings. Follow the hedge line, it goes a long way, if you stay low they won't be able to see you. About three miles west there is a large area of forest. If you're lucky the people there will help you, now go quickly.'

Ernie listened but had no idea if the farmer was with them or against them. He looked at Ruth hoping for some acknowledgement on their situation. Her half smile reassured him and she gave him the farmer's instructions.

'We have to go now, keep low behind the outbuilding and follow the hedge.' Ernie nodded and turned back to the farmer.

'Thank you for everything.' Ernie opened the door just a fraction to check their escape route. He glanced back at Ruth.

'Ready?'

'As I'll ever be,' she replied.

'Right, let's go.'

'One second,' said Ruth. She turned back to the farmer and quickly ran over to him, reaching up she gently pulled his face towards her and kissed him on the cheek, 'Thank you Gerhard, you are a good man I hope after the war your sons come home safely.' In his heart he felt the sincerity of her words. His eyes filled with tears as he fought back the emotion, 'Go quickly, there is no time.'

As fast as their legs would carry them, staying low, they dashed across the yard down the side of the stable. Once behind the buildings and out of sight of the road, they made their way along the hedges between the fields; quickly disappearing into the countryside.

Back at the farm Gerhard Meyer peered through the window into the back yard where a canvas backed troop carrier pulled up just yards from his back gate, immediately followed by a black staff car. Two by two, heavily armed troopers jumped from the tail gate and formed up in two lines. The driver of the staff car got out and opened the rear door. First out of the car was Hauptmann Fleischer closely followed by Kohl. As the farmer watched from his window he thought what a peculiar partnership: a straight backed tower of a man followed by a rotund little man who appeared to be not much bigger than a child.

Fleischer being the military side of the partnership looked at Kohl in disgust as the little man shouted, 'Search all the buildings immediately,' without any discussion.

'Herr Kohl,' said Fleischer, 'can I bring it to your attention that this is the home of a German citizen? A simple knock at the door would achieve the same result and probably get more cooperation.'

Without even making eye contact Kohl replied, 'My dear Hauptmann Fleischer, in the Gestapo we have a way of getting results fast and on this occasion speed is of the essence.' With that Kohl advanced at speed towards the farmhouse followed by two troopers. Fleischer shook his head and gritted his teeth; under his breath he said, 'Little shit, I'll have my day with you.'

Seeing them approaching the back door, the farmer went out to meet them.

'Good morning sir, how can I help you?'

'Heil Hitler,' said Kohl raising his right arm.

'Heil Hitler,' responded the farmer somewhat less enthusiastically. Fleischer caught up and interrupted the conversation; he wasn't going to be bullied by this man like so many others.

'Good day sir, we are looking for two escaped prisoners, a man and a woman. Have you seen anyone around your farm?'

The farmer raised a hand to his mouth and pondered a moment, 'There are a lot of people on the road, but no one has been here for a good week.'

Fleischer nodded, 'You don't mind if we just search the outbuilding? They are both dangerous and we wouldn't want to leave without insuring your safety.'

'Certainly,' said the farmer, 'feel free.'

Kohl, as suspicious as ever, stared at the man; the farmer could feel the little man's eyes boring into him and the farmer swallowed hard.

'I am thirsty,' said Kohl, 'Could we come in and get liquid refreshment of some kind?' Kohl watched closely for his reaction.

'Yes sir, I haven't got much but you are welcome to what I have.'

'Water will be sufficient,' said Kohl still watching him like a hawk. The farmer held the door back, Kohl stepped in followed by Fleischer. As soon as the farmer closed the door he realised his mistake, the table was set for four.

Trying to divert attention away from the table the farmer said, 'I have a little schnapps, if you would like something to warm you.' Kohl, with his hands held firmly behind his back, peered out of the window.

Fleischer smiled, 'That is kind of you sir.'

'Water will suffice,' interrupted Kohl.

'Sorry, let me clear this away.' Quickly the farmer gathered the plates and brushed the crumbs off the table hoping they hadn't noticed. 'Please take a seat.' With a tea towel he brushed the seat of the chair for Fleischer.

'Thank you, may I ask your name sir?'

'Meyer, sir, Gerhard Meyer. My two sons are at the Eastern front.' Kohl turned round, the farmer took two glasses from the side board and placed them on the table. He picked up a schnapps bottle with probably just enough for two shots left in it and pulled out the cork.

'How many people live here at present Herr Meyer?' asked Kohl, rocking from heel to toe on his feet.

'Just me and my wife Edith, she is taking a nap. The war has paid its toll on her.'

'Umm,' said Kohl. As the farmer poured the snaps Kohl said, 'That is strange, then why would you set the table for four?'

The farmer's hand could be seen to be visibly shaking. Once he had poured the drinks he put the bottle down. Kohl and Fleischer stared at him. Thinking on his feet he said, 'That is my wife, she always lays the table as if the boys were home. As I said the war is paying its toll on her.' Fleischer shook his head with a sympathetic grimace on his face.

Kohl waited a few seconds then said, 'I don't believe you Herr Meyer.' Kohl picked up the glass of schnapps and downed it in one. Slamming the glass on the table he strode over to the back door and vigorously pulled it open. A group of four soldiers were standing a few yards from the back door. 'You men search the house?' He stood back and the soldiers ran in. Fleischer jumped to his feet trying to defend the farmer,

'Herr Kohl, do you not think this is harsh? Herr Meyer's explanation seems satisfactory.'

'My dear Hauptmann Fleischer, I have been doing this job long enough to know he is lying through his teeth, now please let me do my job.'

Fleischer turned to the farmer and looked into his eyes. The farmer immediately broke eye contact, and at that moment Fleischer knew Kohl was right.

'I am disappointed with you sir,' said Fleischer, he shook his head turned and walked out. Not wanting any part of Kohl's bullying tactics, he made his way back to the staff car.

The soldiers left no stone unturned. On Kohl's orders they showed no respect for the farmer's belongings, turning over beds and pulling out drawers, finally finding their way to the room where Edith Meyer, even with all the rumpus, slept soundly.

'Get up,' shouted one of the soldiers, waking her with a start.

'Gerhard, is that you?' Pulling the blanket off her they grabbed her arms and pulled her to her feet. With that the screaming started. At the top of her voice she called for help, 'Gerhard, help me, help me!' Her husband had remained calm in the kitchen, sticking to his story. At the sound of his wife's cries, he became like a man possessed, charging through the house and into his wife's bedroom. Seeing the two soldiers manhandling his beloved Edith finished lighting an already short fuse. His many years working the land had made him a very strong individual; even two relatively young men were no match for him. He grabbed the first soldier by his shoulders and literally threw him across the room, he bounced off the wardrobe in a crumpled heap. The second threw a punch which glanced off his chin; in his current state of rage it barely bothered him. He grabbed the soldier by the throat with both hands and squeezed. The soldier clawed at the farmer's hands in an attempt to release his grip, but it was futile. Meanwhile, hearing the rumpus in the bedroom, Kohl showing no pressure opened the back door and called out to another group of soldiers, 'Quickly you men, in here.' With weapons at the ready, they dashed through the house, another few seconds and the soldier would have been dead. The first soldier in the room raised the butt of his rifle and struck the farmer in the back of the head; that was the last thing he could remember before everything became dark.

He didn't know how long he had been unconscious; as he opened his eyes the room was spinning. He took a deep breath, closed his eyes again, and shook his head. As the room stopped spinning he felt a searing pain, then he remembered the blow to the back of his head; that explained it. He was sat on a chair facing the kitchen table with his hands bound behind his back. Directly in front of him his wife sat with her hands on her face, apparently unable to cope with what was going on around her. He tried to separate his hands, but they were well and truly secured.

A voice from behind him said, 'The penalty for harbouring escaped prisoners is death.' The farmer again struggled with his bindings. Two hands were suddenly placed on his shoulders. 'Please, please my friend, you are wasting your time trying to escape.' Kohl stepped round to face him, 'Why on earth would a man in your position, with two fine sons fighting for our beloved country help fugitives of our cause?'

'I,' SLAP, the back of Kohl's hand hit him just below his right eye. In a sadistic voice he said, 'I didn't ask you to speak, yet.' His wife already in tears reached out with her hand, 'Put your hand down Frau Meyer or you will also be bound.'

'Don't,' said the farmer, in a futile attempt to reassure his wife.

SLAP, before he could even get a sentence out Kohl's hand hit him again in the face. 'You are not listening to me.' Kohl walked round the table so he was facing the farmer and placed his hands on Edith's shoulders, 'Now I know you are a reasonable man Herr Meyer, and I don't want to cause you any undue pain and suffering, but I really need to catch these two individuals and quickly.' He squeezed the old woman's shoulders, her body tensed, obviously in pain.

'Take your hands off her you no good scum, you are a disgrace to our people.'

'Temper, temper! It appears I have found your soft spot.' Kohl went over to the window and tapped the glass, immediately two troopers came through the door.

'Hold the lady's hands on the table for me.' One either side of her they grabbed her wrists, and held her hands firmly forcing them palm down on the table. Kohl went over to a drawer by the sink and pulled it open. Rummaging through, first he picked up a marble rolling pin and weighed it in his hand. Wrinkled his nose and shook his head, as if to say to himself, no. Then he picked up a small meat cleaver, a sadistic smile etched across his face. He closed the draw and walked back over to the table.

'I will ask you once and once only. If I think you are telling me the truth, we will leave and that will be the end of it. If you don't I will start with your wife's little finger and I think you know the rest,' he grinned.

With a look of horror on his face, the farmer begged, 'Please do what you like to me, but my wife is blind and ill, she can do you no harm.' Even the two troopers holding the woman's wrists couldn't believe what was happening before their eyes.

'Tell me everything you know about the escaped prisoners.' The farmer didn't want to, but had no allegiance to the young couple and he wasn't going to risk his dear wife enduring such torture.

'They went west, early this morning, all they did was eat some food and left, that's all I know.' Kohl shook his head,

'I said I would only ask you once.'

The farmer screamed at him, 'IT'S THE TRUTH I TELL YOU.' Kohl put the tip of the cleaver on the table and rested the blade over Edith's little finger. He looked at the farmer; his eyes looked as if they were going to pop out of his head. With one fast sharp movement he brought the blade down, severing the old lady's finger just above the knuckle. Her screams could be heard all around the farm.

'YOU BASTARD!' shouted the farmer, 'I HAVE TOLD YOU EVERYTHING I KNOW.'

Kohl positioned the blade next to Edith's ring finger on the same hand and raised the blade.

'I'M TELLING YOU THE TRUTH FOR GOD'S SAKE MAN.' Kohl stopped and put the blade down. As calmly as anything he said, 'I believe you are, but I had to be sure.' The soldier let go of Edith's wrists and she immediately pulled her hand close to her chest, sobbing. 'Take him outside, keep him bound then come back for the old woman,' the soldiers pulled the farmer's arms high up behind his back. He grimaced in pain as they half dragged him out of the farm house. Kohl followed, they threw him face down in the dirt and went back for his wife.

Once she was outside, sitting on the floor beside her husband, Kohl said, 'You will remember the day you became a traitor of the Fatherland.' There were at least a dozen soldiers standing in the farmyard. Kohl simply turned to them and said, 'Burn the place.' At first they hesitated, Kohl scanned his eyes over them, making eye contact with as many as possible.

'Do you have a problem with following orders?'

'No sir,' came a collective reply.

The farmer could do nothing but watch the home he had worked all his life to maintain, burn before his very eyes. Hauptmann Fleischer watched from the road, his heart dropped. This wasn't why he joined the military. At that moment, he was ashamed of his fellow countrymen.

'Sounds like he was a half decent bloke this farmer,' said Alex, briefly interrupting the old veteran.

'Yes,' said Ernie, 'he didn't have to help us, and when that patrol turned up he could have just handed us over to them.' Ernie smiled, 'My Ruth was really taken by his kindness.' The old man thought to himself for a moment, 'I always wondered what happened after we left, we got best part of a mile away. I decided to stop, just for a minute, to give Ruth a breather. Back in the direction of the farm a big plume of smoke went up, a fire of some kind, we just hoped it wasn't near the farm. Anyway we did as he said and kept to the hedgerows going west. It was a lot further than he said; talk about a farmer's mile.

It was nearly a two hour walk before they saw the edge of the forest. The going underfoot was really hard, and having to stay stooped a lot of the time didn't help.

'Not far now darling,' said Ernie. 'Once we are in the tree line you can rest a little.' Ernie, ever-vigilant, kept looking all around for any signs of the soldiers from the farm house. 'So far so good,' said Ernie peering behind them over a particularly high section of hedgerow.

Finally they reached the treeline; they both felt a lot safer being under cover of the trees. Ruth gave out a large sigh and slumped down at the base of a tree, 'My feet are killing me,' she said, slipping off a shoe. Ernie looked back over the land they had just crossed. In the distance the sky was black with smoke, neither of them wanted to say it but in their hearts they knew it was the farmhouse. Ernie just hoped the old couple had not been harmed.

After about ten minutes Ernie said it was time to go.

Ruth looked up, 'Yes, I know, just get my shoes back on.' Her feet were both cold and swollen; after a short struggle she managed to get them on. Ernie put out both hands and pulled her to her feet, 'OK?'

He lead the way through the dark, dense forest, no real path to speak of, their goal being just to keep moving and put as much distance between themselves and the patrol as possible.

They had been walking for approximately twenty minutes, when out of the corner of Ernie's eye he saw what he thought was the figure of a man some fifty yards or so to his left. He didn't want to frighten Ruth, and he wasn't really sure if the trees were playing tricks on him, so he remained silent but kept extra vigilant. A few minutes later, off to his right he saw another. This time he was sure.

'Just keep walking and try not to look alarmed, we are being watched.' Ruth instantly tensed and began to panic. 'Calm down,' said Ernie, taking her hand,' they might not be interested in us, let's just keep walking and hope they leave us alone.' Within minutes there were at least seven or eight figures now completely surrounding them, and they were drawing closer. Suddenly from behind a tree not five yards in front of them a man stepped out holding a pistol at arm's length, aiming directly at Ernie. His face was covered in dirt; his clothing looked like it was held together with pieces of rope. In German he said:

'Stop and raise your hands or I will shoot.'

Their hearts felt as if they were going to burst out of their chests. In seconds there was a perimeter of men all around them with rifles, shotguns a whole variety of weapons. All of them appeared to have been living rough for some time. The man with the pistol and two other's kept their weapons fixed on Ernie and Ruth while the others stepped forward and started frisking their clothing. Trying not to spook them they kept their arms as high as possible showing no retaliation.

'What are you doing in our forest?' asked the man with the pistol. Ernie just looked blankly back at him, he hadn't a clue what he had said. Ruth replied,

'He can't talk.' The man pointed the gun at Ruth's head.

'I wasn't talking to you.' Ernie stepped in front of Ruth, in English he said,

'Please we mean you no harm.' The others raised their guns and took one step back, shocked at hearing an English voice. Bad move, thought Ernie, now they are definitely going to shoot us. Thinking on her feet Ruth said,

'A friend sent us this way, a man called Gerhard Meyer, he's a local farmer.' The man with the pistol lowered his gun and the others followed suit.

'Gerhard is a friend of mine, a good man, how do you know him?' 'He fed and sheltered us, we had to escape a patrol that turned up at his farm. We fear the worst for him and his wife.'

'Did they follow you?'

'I don't think so, we kept a good look out behind us,' Ruth was trying her best to reassure them. 'He said the people in the forest would help us.'

'And why would we do that?'

'Because maybe you are good men also,' she was starting to get somewhere. The man nodded his head and half smiled,

'Blindfold them.' As the men pulled rags from their pockets Ernie looked alarmed. In English Ruth said to Ernie,

'Don't worry, I think they are taking us to their camp.' Ernie nodded.

Neither of them could see as they set off through the woods, each stood behind a man with their hands firmly placed on their shoulders.

It seemed as if they had been walking for hours, but that was probably due to the disorientation from the blindfolds; it was actually no more than twenty or thirty minutes. The temporary blindness had made their hearing quite acute. Nearby they could hear what sounded like children playing. Suddenly the men guiding them stopped. Taking their hands from their shoulders they waited to be told what to do. From behind, someone unfastened and removed their blindfolds. They couldn't believe their eyes; it was like a small village deep within the forest. The small shed-like structures were ramshackle, but no doubt served a purpose on a cold winter night. There must have been more than fifty people and a handful of children played blind man's bluff, to the annoyance of the smallest and probably the youngest member who was failing miserably to catch them. A thickset man with a large greying beard came over carrying a shotgun, with a large bandolier of shotgun shells slung across his shoulder. Like the others, he also looked like he hadn't washed for some time. His clothes looked as if they had been made out of old sacks.

'So you're friends of Gerhard?' asked the man without introducing himself.

'Yes,' said Ruth, 'he told us you would help us on our journey.'

'And what is your journey exactly?' Ruth thought for a moment, was she telling them too much? What the hell she thought: we have nothing to lose now.

'We are heading west, towards the British and American forces. This is my friend, he is British, he was injured in battle and somehow ended up in a German hospital, we think the patrol was hunting for us.' The man looked at Ernie and thought for a while then he said,

'You could have put us in grave danger coming here. If they have followed you and they come into the woods,' he shook his head, turning round and looked around at his community. 'It's taken us almost two years to build what we have here, there are Jews, religious abstainers, some men who deserted for their own reasons, we don't ask why.'

He turned to his comrades, their eyes were firmly fixed on him waiting for a decision. Ernie and Ruth could see they trusted him implicitly.

'Gustav,' he said, 'take two men, go back where we found them; keep hidden, any sign they were followed report back as quickly as possible.' He turned to a man stood on his right. 'Heinz, you also take two men, go to the western border of the forest.' He placed his hand on Heinz's shoulder, 'stay alert my friend, the patrol know they are going west. If they anticipate their actions they will have gone round the forest in their trucks and be waiting, probably hiding in the fields the other side of the treeline.'

Heinz said nothing, just nodded, pointed at two men and all three of them turned and ran off into the forest. The man with the beard turned to Ruth,

'Our friend Gerhard provided food from his farm when we first took shelter in the forest. That is why we help you, no other reason,' Ruth gave an understanding nod.

'Now, you may eat and drink something warm with us, and then we will blindfold you again and take you to the western edge of the forest, after that you're on your own.'

'Thank you,' said Ruth, 'that is already more than we expected.'

They were taken to a large open fire; with skewers of what looked like skinned rabbits suspended above. Occasional droplets of fat fell onto the open flames causing the fire to spit. Neither Ernie nor Ruth was very hungry, having eaten at the farmhouse, but not knowing where there next meal was coming from, they took every opportunity they could to fill their stomachs.

Exactly as the man with the beard had said, Kohl had anticipated the way they intended to make their escape. After they had left the farm in flames and without consulting Fleischer, Kohl directed the drivers of both the staff car and the troop carrier to take the road round the edge of the forest. The western edge of the forest had been cleared for farmland, producing a straight line of trees for nearly a mile.

It was a lot of land to marshal but Kohl was convinced, with just a little luck, this is where he would intercept them. As the vehicles sped towards their ambush location, the atmosphere in the staff car was sombre. Fleischer couldn't bring himself to look at Kohl let alone talk to him. Kohl sensed the displeasure of his companion and decided to break the ice.

'My dear Hauptmann Fleischer, I know you do not agree with my methods, but I assure you they get results.' Fleischer could feel his anger building up inside; if he didn't air his views he would probably shoot the man. He turned and looked Kohl straight in the eye.

'My dear Herr Kohl,' he sneered, 'if burning down the house of a member of the German public is the way of achieving your goals, I think I will pass.' Kohl went on the offensive, raising his voice.

'He forfeit his position as a member of the German public when he sheltered and collaborated with the enemy.'

'Nonsense,' snapped Fleischer equally as loud,

'They probably spoke perfect German and told him lie after lie to get what they wanted from him.' Kohl laughed unsympathetically, 'Well it didn't take long for me to get what I wanted out of them.' The expression on Kohl's face was that of a sadistic bully. Fleischer turned away and gritted his teeth. How he restrained himself from hitting the pint sized thug, he didn't know.

The driver who had been slowly sinking in his seat as the argument progressed suddenly sat up straight and turned to look over his shoulder.

'Approaching the tree line you requested Herr Kohl.'

'Good, good,' replied Kohl, 'reduce your speed, keep going till you are half way along the tree line then pull over, keep the vehicle as quiet as possible.'

The staff car reduced its speed to 20 mph; the troop carrier did the same and fell in close behind. All eyes were on the forest, the slightest movement in the trees and the soldiers would have been out of the back of the lorry in double time, pursuing their prey. After approximately 800 yards there was a small inlet in the trees. Kohl instructed the driver to pull in, it was the best cover they were going to get. As soon as they were off the road and the engines were turned off, two by two the soldiers leapt from the back of the troop carrier, awaiting their orders.

Unknown to Kohl and his patrol, less than 50 yards before they pulled into the small inlet the three men, sent to scout the western border line of the forest, lay face down in dense brush. Watching and waiting for their next move, once they had an approximate number and arms count they slowly backed off into the woods, disappearing as stealthily as they had arrived. Once they were at a safe distance, they ran as fast as their legs would carry them back to the camp. Within 10 minutes they were back. As they entered the camp people stopped to look, obviously concerned as to why they were in such a great hurry. The man with the beard went straight over. Panting to get his breath Heinz reported what they had seen,

'Soldiers on the west treeline twenty maybe twenty five, well-armed. Got a feeling they are here for them.' He nodded his head towards Ernie and Ruth sat by the camp fire. The man with the beard, obviously concerned, looked at the people all around.

'Listen everyone, we knew this could happen. With a little luck they will stay on the edge of the forest.' He looked into the eyes of some of the women and children, sensing their fear. 'But we can't take that chance,' rubbing his beard with his thumb and index finger he thought for a moment then said. 'We go with our original plan, a small group of us will take those two to the edge of the forest. The rest including the women and children will break camp and go deeper. Take what you can, and hide what you can't carry.'

Everyone stood in silence looking at their leader, he gave a half smile and said,

'Don't worry we have survived this long.' A look of doubt was etched on their faces. Like a true leader, he took control. 'Come along people, let's move.'

As if a switch had been thrown, they all went into action, every man woman and child appeared to have a purpose. Ruth had been listening intently on what was happening and quickly explained to Ernie. The bearded man walked over to them and from his waist band he pulled out a Luger pistol, turned the handle towards Ernie and offered it to him. Ernie looked at the gun and hesitated for moment, then cautiously accepted the weapon. Looking at Ruth he said,

'And my name is Leon, Leon Neuburger,' Ruth smiled instantly realising his surname was Jewish.

'Very pleased to meet you Leon,' said Ruth.

'Likewise Fraulein, now let's get moving, we haven't much time.'

'So they were Jews,' said Alex.

'No not all of them,' replied Ernie, 'but I don't mind saying I was surprised to find out who the leader was. They all had their own reasons for being in that forest. At that moment in time we were just glad they were. We wouldn't have stood a chance against that patrol without them.' Ernie shook his head slightly, looking very thoughtful he said, 'We had a lot of close ones, but I think I can safely say, without them we would have died that day, or been taken back to Berlin to be interrogated by the Gestapo, I think it would have been better to have died in the forest than that.' Alex sat up straight,

'What happened then?'

'Well,' said Ernie, 'we set off through the woods. Ruth, me and ten of the men including the leader, Leon.'

Within fifteen minutes the area was unrecognisable as an encampment, let alone one that had been used for the last eighteen months. Everything they could carry was in backpacks or fastened around their waists. They all lined up waiting for the next order, their faces etched with worry. Leon glanced around the camp, as if he was inspecting their handiwork. Once he was happy he turned and faced them,

'I want ten volunteers, well nine as I'm going. Heinz I need you as you know the whereabouts of the patrol, hopefully we can avoid a confrontation.' Heinz stepped forward,

'Ready when you are.'

'Thank you,' said Leon. He looked at the rest of the group, slowly and hesitantly one by one they raised their hands. When he had enough raised hands he said,

'Let's move, we travel light, nothing but weapons and ammunition. Give everything else you have to the others for safekeeping. The rest of you men take the women and children deep into the forest, we will come and find you when it's safe.' He turned to Ruth and Ernie, 'Fraulein let's get you and your companion out of our forest.' The men double checked their weapons. In single file, with Heinz leading the way, they cautiously set off west through the dense woodland.

They had been walking a little over ten minutes. Ernie and Ruth were almost at the rear of the file with the exception of Leon and another man who had been given the task of staying a little way back to guard their rear. In a quiet voice Leon said,

'When you clear the forest if you keep going due west, you will at some stage have to cross the river Elbe. It's a very deceiving river, the current can be treacherous. I wouldn't try to wade over or swim it, wait till nightfall and steal a boat. Our sources tell us the bridges are still teeming with retreating soldiers. Ruth listened intently, trying to take in as much information as possible. 'It's only a matter of weeks, even days, before the British and Americans end this madness.'

'Thank you,' said Ruth, 'we will take your advice.'

'You're not far from Magdeburg, about fifteen or twenty miles, I'd avoid it. What's left of it will be swarming with soldiers dug in for a last stand. Once that falls there will be no stopping them, they will be in Berlin the same day and with the Russians attacking the city from the east, it will be all over very quickly.'

Up ahead Heinz suddenly stopped and dropped to one knee, one by one all the men followed suit.

'Stay here,' said Leon. Keeping low he moved up to the front of the line. Kneeling beside Heinz he said,

'What have you seen my friend?' Heinz slowly shook his head,

'I don't know but I have a bad feeling.' The forest ahead thinned out considerably almost into a complete clearing, followed by what was possibly the darkest densest part of the wood.

'It's too quiet,' said Heinz, 'If I was setting up a trap this is where it would be.' Both the men stared silently into the woodland ahead, looking for the slightest movement or sign of life. After what felt like an age but was actually no more than a few minutes, Heinz broke the silence by taking a deep breath.

'I'm getting the jitters,' Leon tapped him on the shoulder,

'We all are my friend, we all are.' With that Heinz stood up and turned to the file of men behind him, he raised his hand to signal they were moving on. No sooner had half the men stood up when all hell broke loose. Muzzle flashes from the other side of the clearing showered the surrounding area; bullets, bark and branches exploded all around them. Heinz was the first to be hit, two, three or even four bullets slammed into his back spinning him around like a top. Blood splattered over the two men immediately behind him. Ernie reacted by pushing Ruth flat on her face and using himself as a shield on top of her. Gathering their wits, those who could opened fire in the direction of the still unseen enemy.

Ernie, being an experienced soldier, knew there would be a short lapse in the mayhem while they reloaded. Handheld automatic weapons release ammunition at an astounding rate, but not for long. The woodsmen, with their rifles, pistols and shotguns kept up a good counter offensive, but after the first hail of bullets Ernie knew it was in vain; they were massively outgunned. The woodsmen were now spread out in a straight line firing indiscriminately at the trees in front of them. This was probably Ernie and Ruth's only chance to escape. With the pistol Leon had given him drawn he grabbed Ruth's shoulder. Survival was all that was on his mind,

'Stay low, follow me.' With their chests virtually on the ground they backed off. Ernie expected the German soldiers to flank them, to try and catch them in a cross fire. Again the unseen enemy opened fire. One by one the woodsmen were being cut down. Some just lay on the floor or hid behind trees, never having experienced combat before, their bodies froze with fear. Seeing this, their leader waited for the next lapse in fire. Then with a pistol in each hand Leon got to his feet and ran straight at them. Like a mad man he screamed at the top of his voice as he ran through the clearing, firing both guns as he went. Seeing this, those that could still stand found courage and followed him into the trees, screaming like banshees and firing at anything that moved.

Ernie and Ruth by now had backed off quite some distance. Trying to evaluate their situation, Ernie looked straight at Ruth. Her face said it all, she was petrified. He grabbed her shoulders a little more roughly than she would have liked.

'Listen to me, and do exactly as I say.' Ruth nodded, her mouth was slightly ajar, her breathing rapid and, as he looked into her eyes he saw that her pupils were extremely dilated, a clear sign she was in shock. He loosened his grip and rubbed the top of her arms,

'Keep it together now,' she gave him a hesitant nod, trying to reassure her he said, 'We are going to make it, understand?' She didn't reply.

'Understand?' he repeated.

Like flicking on a light switch her eyes focused on him.

'Yes,' she said. Ernie quickly scanned the surrounding area,

'We have to break right, stay low and just keep going, I'll be right behind you.' Ruth didn't need telling twice, the fight or flight response was well and truly engaged. As they ran, some distance behind they heard the occasional discharge of automatic weapons, but it didn't sound as if it was getting any closer. Within a few minutes all they could hear was the snapping of twigs underfoot as they once again made their escape, Ernie frequently checking behind for any sign they were being pursued.

They had to assume all the woodsmen had been killed, it was just them now, and survival was top of the agenda.

Back at the clearing, Kohl and his patrol had killed six of the woodsman including Leon. The other four, all looking worse for wear, were sat in a line surrounded by soldiers. Kohl walked up and down in front of them shaking his head.

'Call yourself Germans; you are a disgrace to the Fatherland.' Pensively he rubbed his hand along his jaw line, and then pointed to the woodsman at the end.

'You, stand up,' the man was bleeding heavily from a bullet wound to his shoulder. Leaning to his good side he struggled to get to his feet, he wasn't even half way up Kohl stepped closer and kicked him in the shin, 'Get up I said.'

Two soldiers behind stepped forward, grabbed him by the scruff of the neck and yanked him up. The man grimaced in pain from the pressure exerted on his shoulder. Kohl drew a pistol from his right hand pocket and pointed it at the man's forehead.

'Where are the man and woman that entered the forest earlier today?'

'I don't know,' BANG. He shot the man. Blood spurted from a perfectly round hole in the middle of his forehead. The man's lifeless body collapsed in a heap, everyone was in shock, the German soldiers couldn't believe what they had just witnessed. Hauptmann Fleischer, who was standing some way back, could see the way this was going. He turned and walked back through the woods in the direction of the vehicles.

The remaining three woodsmen lowered their heads hoping in some way that they would not be next.

'You,' said Kohl pointing his weapon at the next man in the row. He had a bullet wound in his thigh. Refusing to show any weakness in front of such a tyrant, he struggled to his feet, not allowing the soldiers to assist him. Kohl looked straight into the man's eyes then raised his gun. 'I am going to ask you the same question, before you speak I want you to think very hard, and be careful with your answer, do you understand?' The man nodded, 'Where are the man and woman that entered the forest earlier today?' The man was quiet for a few seconds then he smiled and said,

'Fuck you.' BANG. Another body dropped in a lifeless heap. The soldiers were getting visibly agitated by Kohl's actions. A few started to back off; Kohl sensed this and raised his weapon in their direction. At the top of his voice he shouted,

'STAND STILL WHILE I AM INTEROGATING THESE TRAITORS!' The soldiers swallowed hard and stood their ground. All eyes stared at Kohl, he looked at the third man. Gesturing up and down with the barrel of his pistol he said, 'You, stand.' The man no more than about twenty five was shaking, at some stage in the last few minutes he had urinated in fear, as the front of his trousers were soaking wet. He didn't appear to have any bullet wounds but his face was heavily bruised and bleeding, probably from the butt of a weapon as he was over powered. Kohl looked him up and down, shook his head and sucked his lips,

'Disgusting,' he paused for a second or two then said, 'Well I think you know the format.' Kohl again raised his weapon and pointed it at the man's face.

'They were with us right up till the fighting began,' blurted out the man in a frantic attempt to save his own skin. The fourth man slumped to his side clutching his stomach; he had been hit two or three times in the torso and knew he hadn't long left. The Gestapo tyrant had got the information he required. He closed his eyes and waited for the inevitable. Kohl ignored him and continued questioning the other man.

'So where are they now?'

'They must have ran back into the woods.' Kohl turned and walked two or three yards, peering deep into the dense woodland. He took a deep breath and exhaled as he turned to face the man,

'So really that is all the information you can give me.'

'Yes sir, I don't know any more,' Kohl raised his weapon and just like the others shot him in the head, BANG. Without pausing he stepped over the man's body, the fourth man still lay on his side curled up in the foetal position with his eyes closed. Bending down slightly he put the gun close to the man's temple and pulled the trigger, BANG. He looked at the group of stunned soldiers stood before him. As he slid his pistol into his pocket he said,

'I think our business here is concluded, they will not come back this way; back to the vehicles. We must intercept them before nightfall.' The soldiers, as a group, turned and headed back, there wasn't a man amongst them who would dare question his authority.

Kohl instructed the men to get back to the truck as fast as possible. The driver of the truck who had been left behind on guard saw them coming, quickly he climbed into the truck cab. Hauptmann Fleischer was leaning against the staff car smoking a cigarette, looking disheartened. The soldiers climbed into the back of the truck and as Kohl approached the staff car Fleischer stood up dropped his cigarette and ground it into the floor with his boot.

'No prisoners then,' said Fleischer. Kohl was about to get into the car, but he stopped and looked up at him.

'My dear Hauptmann Fleischer, why on earth would there be prisoners?' Fleischer stared straight through him,

'They were German people.' At the top of his voice Kohl shouted,

'THEY WERE TRAITORS,' realising he had lost his composure he took a handkerchief from his pocket and wiped his mouth. Once again in control he continued,

'They assisted our enemy's escape, if we had taken them back they would have faced a firing squad. Think of it as saving them the anxiety of waiting for the inevitable.'

Fleischer's blood was boiling; he detested the little man with a vengeance. As Fleischer stepped round the front of the car Kohl sensed his anger. Taking one step backwards Kohl put his hand in his pocket and firmly held his gun. Fleischer stepped up close to his face, unaware Kohl was pointing a gun at him in his pocket.

'You're an evil man Kohl, and I don't like you one little bit.' Kohl's finger feathered the trigger of the weapon, waiting for any show of physical violence. Nervously Kohl replied,

'That is your prerogative Hauptmann Fleischer.' It was the first time Fleischer had seen the man look threatened, and it felt good.

'You'll get your comeuppance, whether it's in this world or the next, but you will get it,' said Fleischer peering down at him. Kohl stared straight ahead, not wanting to make eye contact. Once composed Kohl said,

'We are losing time.' Fleischer shook his head, it was like water off a duck's back. Fleischer stepped past him deliberately bumping his shoulder as he went,

'I will be traveling in the truck with the men.' Under his breath Kohl said,

'So be it.' The driver jumped out of the car and opened the back door. Kohl got in and sat back, he squeezed his hands together in an attempt to stop them shaking. In all his years in the gestapo there weren't any men that had stood up to him like that, and lived. The driver sensed the tension and cautiously asked,

'Where to, sir?' Kohl took a deep breath,

'Back the way we came. I have a feeling, they will exit the forest on the north edge. The forest is too big to go south and they won't go the way they came.'

'Yes sir,' said the driver.

The car turned and sped off, keeping to the road along the edge of the forest, closely followed by the truck.

'That was close Ernie,' said Alex perched on the edge of his chair. Most of the old soldier's audience had gone about their business, but Alex was more enthralled than ever.

'We didn't know if they had given up or were on our heels. Either way we had to circle back and then head west. Ruth told me the man called Leon had said we were about twenty miles from a town called Magdeburg. It was actually about 30 miles, and when you're cold and have no food that extra 10 miles makes a big difference. Anyway he told us to avoid the place, said it was swarming with soldiers digging in for a last stand. We didn't know at the time but the Yanks were no more than 40 miles away. That Leon also said the bridges at Magdeburg were still intact, you see we had to cross the Elbe at some stage. It's a hell of a big river, you wouldn't want to swim it, especially at that time of the year, and it was bitter cold. Our priority was to keep moving and avoid that patrol.'

Alex interrupted him, 'Did you ever find out what happened to the men in the forest?'

'No,' said Ernie, 'I felt bad leaving them, but when all the shooting started all I could think about was keeping Ruth safe.' For a few seconds Ernie was lost in his own thoughts then he said, 'I guess that's what happens when you find the right girl.' Both men shared a smile of mutual agreement. 'Anyway,' said Ernie, 'we had to get clear of the woods before nightfall and I hadn't a clue where we were. I didn't tell Ruth but deep down I knew that patrol weren't giving up that easily and I was right.'

Kohl and his patrol headed back the way they had come. A little slower than he would have preferred, but he wanted to observe as much of the tree line as possible on the return journey. His plan was to drop off two men every three or four hundred yards and lie in wait for them to cross the road or at least break out of the tree line. With the resources he had he felt it was the best way to cover such a large area of land. Hauptmann Fleischer sat in the front of the truck; he hadn't said a word to the driver or his men since his confrontation with Kohl. If the truth be known he hoped they never found the so called traitors. All he wanted was to rid himself of this tyrant of a man once and for all.

Ernie and Ruth pushed on through the dense forest, occasionally being startled by a woodland creature eager to avoid their presence. It was already late afternoon, in the denser parts of the wood the light was fading, accompanied by the falling temperature. They had no more than a few hours to escape the forest; with no food or shelter it was the last place they wanted to spend the night. Ernie had taken the lead, with nothing more than his hands to clear the branches it was hard going. He stopped for a moment and looked back at Ruth. The sheer pressure they were under was showing on her face. Trying to raise her spirits a little, Ernie said,

'I don't think it's that far now.' Ruth in a state of exhaustion dropped to her knees.

'Can we rest for a while I'm exhausted?' Ernie didn't want to; the only thing they would get from stopping was cold. But after looking into her face for a second or two he said,

'Alright but not for long, once it gets dark in here we will go round in circles.' Ruth got off her knees, walked over to a nearby tree and slumped down with her back against the trunk.

Ernie walked over and sat down beside her. He took hold of her hands and rubbed them between his in an attempt to keep both their circulations going, it was already close to freezing. From all his exertions he felt the sweat on his back start to freeze; it sent a shiver down his spine. He looked at Ruth and attempted a reassuring smile, but it was hard.

'We have to keep moving don't we?' asked Ruth. Ernie just looked at her and gave a knowing nod. Trying to put on a brave face Ruth said, 'Right then let's. Ernie abruptly interrupted her.

'Shush,' raising one hand and turning his head sharply to the left. In the distance and getting louder the sound of a truck engine filled their ears. At first they didn't know whether to run back into the forest or just hide. They were obviously very close to the road. Hopefully if it was the patrol they would go straight past and they would be able to continue heading west. They had to go forward and take a look. Cautiously they moved in the general direction of the engine sound. As the forest started to thin out, Ernie spotted them. The truck had stopped by the edge of the tree line and two soldiers had climbed out and were stood at the rear. Ruth turned her head slightly to one side to try and make out what they were saying, but they were just a little too far away. Then the soldiers in turn raised a hand to the men in the back of the truck and it drove on. Both the soldiers moved off the road and sat down leaning against a tree. Ernie watched the truck till it disappeared round a small bend. Then, from some way down the road. He heard the brakes squeal as the vehicle came to a halt. The penny dropped.

'They're placing guards along the treeline,' said Ernie. He glanced back at the two men. 'They want us to make a break for it,' Ernie went very quiet.

'What are we going to do?'

'I'm going to have to take them out.' Ruth quickly turned and looked at him.

'You are joking of course.'

Ernie made no reply or eye contact. She knew he wasn't.

As the light started to fail Ernie knew it was now or never, his problem was that the two soldiers were too close together. There was no way he could take one out without the other getting involved or sounding the alarm. If he used his pistol the rest of the patrol would be on them in minutes, somehow he needed a distraction but what?

'Don't do anything stupid,' said Ruth, 'I would sooner we take our chances in the forest than risk being captured or worse.'

Suddenly one of the soldiers stood up and stretched, he said something to his companion which he found amusing, flung his weapon onto is back and walked off to his right, going deeper into the forest. This was Ernie's chance, he turned to Ruth,

'Stay here, if you hear gunfire or anything happens to me, go back into the forest and keep going till you find the forest people.' Ruth tried to interrupt him,

'But...'

'No buts,' said Ernie, 'there's no time, just do it.'

Their eyes froze together for a millisecond, 'I love you Ernie White,' she grabbed him and held him tight. Ernie whispered in her ear, 'I love you too, stay hidden.' With that he checked the position of the lone soldier sat against the tree. Keeping very low he moved off to his left, instantly switching into military mode.

As Ruth watched him stealthily disappear into the undergrowth, some thirty or forty yards to their left the German soldier stood tall and looked all around. Unable to put off the call of nature any longer the soldier took his machine gun from his shoulder and leaned it against a tree. He unfastened his trousers, had a final glance around then squatted down. Ernie was closing in behind him, a knife would have been his weapon of choice and the soldier was carrying one on his belt. Trouble was if he tried to take the knife from him the chances were he would call out to his companion or worse still attract the attention of the whole patrol. It had to be fast and instantaneous. In complete silence, and almost on all fours Ernie closed the gap. Like a leopard stalking its prey, five yards, four, three, two he was virtually on top of him. With lightning speed Ernie grabbed the soldier's head and violently twisted it almost 180 degrees, the noise was sickening, as the soldiers neck snapped like a twig. The trauma to his cervical vertebrae must have been immense. The soldier slumped back onto Ernie and was dead before his back hit the ground. Not taking any chances Ernie's clenched fist hit him twice in the throat just below his Adams apple completely crushing his wind pipe. With the soldier's trousers still round his ankles Ernie took the knife from his belt. Still keeping low and looking all around, he grabbed the dead soldier under his armpits and dragged him backwards into some bushes, quickly returning for the machine gun. 'One down,' he said, under his breath. He didn't want to use the machine gun, but if his back was against the wall as a last resort, so be it. Once again he slowly edged through the undergrowth, his slight frame and military training had never been more important to him. Very quickly he caught sight of the second soldier. This wouldn't be as easy; he looked a lot more switched on and alert. Again he needed a distraction, but what, he didn't know.

Ruth's nerves were beginning to get the better of her, she was imagining all sorts of situations Ernie might be in. She couldn't call out but at the same time she couldn't just sit there. Completely dismissing what Ernie had said, slowly and cautiously she started to move forward in the direction he had gone. It had only been ten minutes, but to her it felt like an hour. Almost completely crawling she kept moving forward, stopping every yard or two and crouching up for a better view point. The lone German soldier scanned the forest eager to impress his superiors. Then he saw her, instantly he looked over to where his colleague had gone, and thought,

'He picks his moments to answer the call of nature.' He couldn't call out; he would have to deal with it himself. Seeing the soldier's sudden state of alert, Ernie followed the German's stare.

'Shit,' he said a little louder than he intended, he could see Ruth walking straight into a trap.

He had to move quickly. The soldier looked down the sights of his rifle, he didn't intend to kill her just slow her down a little. Ernie pulled the German dagger from his belt and moved with haste to the rear of the soldier. Fortunately, Ruth lowered down and starting crawling forward.

The soldier kept his aim waiting for his next sighting, he wasn't going to miss. With no thought for his own safety, Ernie ran up behind the German and leapt on his back. His right hand went round the soldier's face and clamped down on his mouth. If he called out or fired his weapon they were done for. His left hand wielded the dagger. The German was a lot bigger than Ernie but the surprise attack had him beat. Ernie plunged the dagger deep into the left side of his neck, more by luck than judgement severing his carotid artery. Blood spurted from the wound; still Ernie clasped his hand firmly across the soldiers mouth. One cry for help and his attack would have been in vain. Pushing the dagger deeper, he waited for the last throes of life to leave the man's body. When he was sure the man was dead, he released his blood stained hand from the around man's face and pulled out the dagger, wiping the blade on the soldier's uniform.

Ernie sat in silence; Alex was concerned by the old veteran's demeanour. He told his audience he had to take out two of the German soldiers, but that was all he said. In his own mind he had relived every last gory detail, as he had done many times, waking in the dead of night drenched in sweat. As a rational considerate human being you can only desensitise yourself so far, and then you just have to live with your thoughts and dreams.

'You OK Ern?' asked Alex.

Suddenly snapping out of his trance-like state Ernie replied, 'Sorry I was miles away, some things are best left in the past.'

'Sure thing old pal,' replied Alex. He had seen first-hand the aftermath of a battle when he served in the Gulf, and could appreciate that some things don't need to be said.

'Anyway,' said Ernie, 'we had to get over that road, we were covered one way by a bend in the road but the other way was wide open. Only thing I could think of was to take the uniforms off the two dead soldiers, at least at a distance if we were spotted it wouldn't be quite so obvious.'

Ruth had been oblivious to the ferocity of Ernie's encounter with the two soldiers. She only saw Ernie when he wanted her to. Quietly under his breath in a half whisper he called her,

'Ruth,' she immediately turned to her right relieved to hear his voice. She moved towards him. As she got closer, a half smile on her face turned to horror when she saw the blood on his hands and clothing.

'Oh my God,' her first thought was that he was injured; Ernie could see this and quickly reassured her.

'Don't worry it's not mine.' a few yards behind him the soldier's lifeless body lay face down blood still flowing from his wounds. Ruth's eyes were still fixed on the blood on his hands.

'I told you to stay put,' said Ernie; he wanted to shout at her but didn't think it appropriate under the circumstances. If she had only known how close she had been to being shot, the thought sent a shudder down his spine. 'Now listen to me, and please do as I say,' Ernie's stare caused Ruth to visibly shrink. 'Stay here, I have to get the uniform off the other soldier, he's only a little way over there, I hid him in the bushes,' Ernie pointed away to his right. 'Just stay hidden,'

Ruth interjected, 'I'll come with you,' he didn't let her finish. Placing his hand on her shoulder he said, 'Please, do as I ask.' Ruth could see she was testing his patience, 'Whatever you say, but be quick.' Ernie smiled,

'I will.' Crouching low, he turned and moved off in the direction of the bushes where he had hidden the soldier's body. Ruth spotted the other soldier a few yards ahead lying face down, the ground around him was stained crimson. Cautiously she moved towards him, as if he was going to spring up at any moment and attack her. Even during her time as a nurse, she had never seen so much blood. Slightly over extending her leg she nudged him, his lifeless form rolled on to his side revealing his face. Suddenly he had an identity, this was someone's son, husband or father, she felt physically sick. She took a deep breath and swallowed hard. Quietly she said to herself,

'Come on now, pull yourself together, it was them or us, now get on with it.' She rolled the soldier onto his back and proceeded to take off his tunic. A couple of minutes later Ernie hurried over. Ruth glanced at him then continued stripping the soldier of his top layer of clothing.

He didn't say anything, but Ernie was very surprised and proud that she had managed to bring herself to do it.

Once they had wiped off as much blood as possible from the uniforms, they put them on. In other circumstances they would have laughed at each other's appearance but comical as they looked, from a distance it would have been hard to distinguish them from the real thing. Ruth put a helmet on her head, it was so big it covered her eyes.

'I can't see a thing,' she said pushing it up. Ernie shook his head and looked around; they had already got the soldier's boots off. He stooped down by the soldier and pulled off the man's socks; hurriedly he rolled them into a ball. He flattened them in the palm of his hands and stood up. Ruth looked a little curious, he lifted the helmet off her head stuffed the socks inside and replaced it, 'Is that better?' Using both hands Ruth positioned it on her head.

'A lot better, thank you.'

Once they were both half dressed in German uniforms and looking absolutely ridiculous, with sub machine guns slung over their shoulders, they moved up towards the clearing at the edge of the road. Just before they came into open view Ernie stopped, 'If you see anyone don't run, just casually walk back into the tree line, you got that?' Ruth nodded, the helmet fell forward over her eyes, Ernie pulled it up. The fear of what they were about to do caused her throat to be so dry she could hardly swallow let alone answer him. Opposite the road the fields were separated by a small hedge; it was a good four hundred yards to any significant cover. Once behind the small hedge they would have to stay very low, virtually on all fours the whole way, but it was the only chance they had.

Ernie stepped out onto the road first, holding the machine gun across his chest. He looked both ways, no sign of anyone. He looked back at Ruth; her small figure dwarfed in the oversize uniform. Ruth was staring straight at him, 'When I say, walk straight across the road and get down behind the hedge, don't hesitate or look around, just do it.' Ruth nodded her head vigorously, Ernie glanced both ways once more, it was all clear, 'Now.'

With the machine gun across her chest, Ruth walked across the road down the small dip and dropped to her knees behind the hedge. Ernie was about to follow when a good six hundred yards down the road a soldier stepped out of the treeline, looking directly at him.

'Shit,' he said under his breath. Without turning to Ruth he said, 'Stay very low and start moving.' Ruth sensed there was something wrong. The soldier in the distance raised his arm; trying to stay calm Ernie took a deep breath and returned the gesture waving his arm twice. Slowly Ernie walked back to the edge of the wood, out of sight from the distant soldier. Ruth was looking back at him, she didn't have to say a word her face was screaming back at him, 'What are we going to do now?' Ernie mouthed, 'Keep going I will catch up,' Ruth looked puzzled. Using the back of his hand in a fanning motion again he mouthed, 'Keep going.' Finally grasping what he meant, although not happy with it, she started along the hedgerow. The helmet kept dropping over her face blocking her vision. 'Enough of this.' She pulled the helmet off her head and dropped it, the machine gun was next and pulling the strap over her head she discarded it. The way it was bouncing around she would risk firing off some rounds and alerting the patrol, or, even worse, accidently shoot herself. If the truth be told, she didn't know how to use it anyway.

Ernie looked down the tree line; the soldier had gone back into the woods. Without the cumbersome equipment, Ruth was making good headway down the field. Here goes, thought Ernie; he walked over the road and got down on the floor facing the woods, machine gun at the ready. If the soldier or any other members of the patrol had seen him, hopefully they would think he was just taking up a better vantage point to observe his section of woodland. He watched and waited. Slowly, he backed into the small ditch, turned and made his way as quickly as he could down the hedgerow in Ruth's direction.

Kohl was becoming impatient; he still hardly knew anything about the fugitives he was chasing. All he was concerned about was his reputation for getting results, whatever the cost. Hauptmann Fleischer had stayed in the cab of the truck, while Kohl had the relative comfort of the staff car. It was starting to get dark; he didn't want to go back to the General empty handed. What to do next? That was the question. His driver was leaning on the front wing of the car; Kohl pulled down the window and called him over.

'Driver,' he immediately came to attention, 'Inform Hauptmann Fleischer we are rounding up the men.'

'Yes sir,' at the double the driver ran over to the truck and informed Fleischer of the pending actions. Fleischer looked over towards the staff car, thinking the sooner this little shit is out of my life the better. The truck driver fired up the engine. With the narrowness of the road what should have been a three point turn turned into a ten point turn. The staff car quickly did the same thing then took up lead position as they slowly drove back down the tree line. In the cab of the truck Fleischer had his foot up on the dash, his eyes fixed on the small figure in the back of the staff car rather than the tree line. As they approached the first drop off point, two soldiers came out of the woods. As they passed, the truck briefly stopped to allow them to clamber over the tail gate. Once on-board one of them banged the side of the truck with the palm of his hand and they moved on. This continued for a considerable distance, by now there were ten men in the back. The next time they pulled up they weren't greeted by their fellow soldiers. Kohl's staff car had already started to move on; the truck driver checked his mirrors and listened for the clamber and bang at the rear of the vehicle.

It did not happen. The driver flashed his lights to attract the attention of the staff car. The staff driver caught the flicker of the lights in his mirror and pulled over immediately. 'What is wrong?' asked Kohl looking up at the driver.

'The truck sir, he is flashing his lights, I think there is something wrong.' Kohl looked over his shoulder. The truck flashed again.

'Back up,' said Kohl. Cautiously the driver reversed the staff car back to the truck. No more than two yards away he came to a halt, then quickly jumped out the car. The truck driver climbed down to meet him.

'Two of the men are missing.'

'You sure?' asked the staff driver.

'I'm sure; I know where I left them.' Quickly he turned and went to the car, Kohl wound down the window. 'Two of the men are missing sir.' Kohl pushed the car door open almost knocking over his driver, quickly climbed out. He turned to the truck driver, 'Fetch the rest of the men, those in the back of the truck search the woods, NOW!' he barked.

'Yes sir,' said both the drivers in unison. They ran round the back of the truck and dropped the tail gate, 'All out, search the woods.'

It didn't take long for them to find the first soldier, partly undressed lying flat on his back, his lifeless eyes staring straight up into the sky. Sheepishly, almost as if they would be disciplined for their find, they called out to Kohl. When he saw the soldier, he clenched his fist and smashed it into the palm of his other hand, 'Imbeciles.' Two of the men began to pick up the body, 'LEAVE HIM,' yelled Kohl louder than was really necessary. All the men in the immediate vicinity stopped and looked over. 'We haven't time to be carting around corpses; it will just slow us down.'

Kohl was pushing his luck, it was one thing to murder a traitor or burn the house of a collaborator but this was a soldier of the Fatherland and their friend.

'Pick him up,' said a voice from behind. Kohl spun round to see who had overruled his authority. Fleischer stood there, his huge frame towering over Kohl, 'Put him in the truck and find the other one.'

Without hesitation the soldiers picked up the body and headed back to the truck. Fleischer stepped uncomfortably close to the smaller tyrant; Kohl went to put his hand in his pocket to search out his hidden pistol, but before he could Fleischer grabbed his hand,

'I wouldn't do that if I were you, you see that last order you gave lost the trust of the men, if there was any left in the first place.' Kohl stared up at him. Suddenly he snatched his arm away turned and called out,

'Find the other man quickly, we are losing valuable time.'

It didn't take them long to find the other man. With the two soldiers' bodies stowed away in the truck, the rest of the men formed up on the road. Fleischer stood looking across the fields deep in thought. The only way he was going to get this man out of his life once and for all was to get the job done. For the sake of his own sanity he decided to work with Kohl. Kohl came and stood beside him.

'They obviously crossed here,' said Fleischer, 'they can't have that much of a head start, maybe a mile or two maximum. I will take ten men on foot; you take the first road due west, drive for three miles, then come back towards me and spread out as best you can. By the time we meet, it will be dark. If we haven't got them by then we will have to resume in the morning.' Kohl thought for a moment. Under the circumstances it was as good a plan as any. Looking straight ahead across the field, he took deep breath. Without turning his head he said, 'Let's get started, time is against us.'

'That was a cold night,' said Ernie sitting up and straightening his back, 'the coldest I could remember for a long time. You see we were both exhausted. We had nothing to eat or drink, our clothes were damp with sweat. Once we got past the first couple of fields there were big hedges dividing up the land. We ran as fast as our feet would carry us. I kept the machine gun but we dumped the uniforms almost as soon as we started running. All we concentrated on was going west, that's all that was on our minds. I knew they were right on our heels but I didn't tell Ruth that at the time, I could see her spirit was already at rock bottom.'

Fleischer quickly selected the ten men who, in his opinion were most up to the task ahead. The others he told to get in the back of the truck. Turning to Kohl, who was actually being quite amicable, he said, 'Don't forget, no more than three miles, they can't have got further than that. I have a feeling they will keep going west.'

'Agreed,' said Kohl. Without another word he turned and walked over to the staff car and got in to the already open back door. The driver had heard everything they had said and didn't hesitate turning the car round. The truck followed suit. As they drove off Fleischer watched for a few seconds then turned to the men.

'Right they have a head start on us, but I selected each man here because I know you won't let me down, let's go.' They spread out and edged down the small embankment into the field. Underfoot they could feel the frost of the night setting in. It would soon be dark, and the task in hand would not be made any easier by the cold and poor visibility. As they walked across the field, they hadn't gone more than a few metres when a soldier walking along the line of the hedge stopped and called out, 'Sir.' He reached down and held up the a soldier's helmet, a little further he picked up the machine gun that Ruth had also discarded and held them high. Fleischer walked over to him and took the helmet, 'Well now at least we know they did pass this way.' Looking ahead he threw the helmet down, like a hound with a scent he carried on walking. Only now his pace quickened.

Ernie and Ruth pushed on, cold and tired but with a renewed faith that they had finally slipped past their adversaries. With the protection of darkness quickly falling around them they felt the odds were starting to stack a little better in their favour. Ernie couldn't ask any more of Ruth, she was already out on her feet. If she could just keep going a few more miles they could stop and get some much needed rest.

Some way ahead, a dim light caught Ernie's eye. By the silhouette in the darkness it was a smallholding of some kind. Ernie knew they had to take exceptional care. Once they got a little closer he could scout the perimeter from a safe distance. Some thirty yards from the main house was the remains of dry stone wall. Ernie and Ruth ran to the wall and got down behind it. Breathing heavily after a good fifty yards sprint they peered over the top, scanning every window and door in turn for the slightest sign of life. Ernie noticed what looked like a military style motorbike leaning against one of the outer walls. The question was how long had it been there, and was its owner home? It could be very useful to them, as a youngster he had fooled around on his brother's motorbikes after school many times, so he was no stranger to handling one and its operation. Without turning to Ruth, Ernie said, 'I'm going to take a closer look, stay here and when I'm sure it's safe I'll signal you.' Ruth had disobeyed him more than once already, something inside told her, 'Not this time.'

She squeezed his arm, 'Be careful.'

With the machine gun in his hands he leapt over the small wall and ran as fast as he could to the motorbike. He crouched down beside it and touched the engine with the back of his hand, stone cold. It hadn't been used for some time. Working his way along the wall, he came to the window with the dim light. He got down low and slowly peered over the top of the sill. It was a kitchen, no sign of anyone in there. He could see a large table and on it a big bloomer style loaf and a hunk of cheese. That will do us he thought to himself. He turned and looked to where he had left Ruth and waved an arm, then lowered his hand as if to say stay low. She didn't need telling twice. Not as athletic, but equally as quick, she jumped over the wall and ran to his position. He pointed through the window and whispered,

'Food,' Ruth nodded. 'Now listen,' said Ernie, 'we are just going to take the food and go. Again Ruth nodded, happy to go along with whatever he said. With the machine gun slung on his back Ernie held the door and latch trying not to make even the slightest noise. He squeezed on the latch, half expecting it to be locked; it gave a loud click and opened. Both their faces grimaced at the noise; all they needed now was rusty door hinges. Ernie slowly pushed the door and fortunately there was no more noise. It was a nice room, the decoration was a little tired and the furniture worn but that was part and parcel of the war. Ernie picked up the bread and tore a piece off and gave it to Ruth; there was a knife next to the cheese so he cut a piece and again passed it to Ruth. Looking around for something to put the food in he opened a cupboard door.

There was a click, a German voice said, 'Don't move.'

In the doorway stood a man, slightly built, about forty-ish, his clothes were a little shabby and he hadn't shaved for a while. Cowering behind him, looking very frightened, was an elderly woman, she must have been seventy at least. Pointing straight out in front of him with two hands he held a Lugar pistol, weapon of choice for most German officers.

'Put down the machine gun and move to the other side of the room.' Ernie hadn't got a clue what he had said.

Ruth raised her hands in a submissive gesture and said, 'We mean no harm, we were hungry.' The man pointed the gun at Ruth then back to Ernie, as if he was trying to decide who was the greater threat. Again but more forcefully, he shouted,

'PUT DOWN THE GUN.' His hands squeezed the pistol a little too tightly for comfort. Ernie understood what he wanted and raised his hands then slowly put his hands on the strap of the machine gun and pulled it over his head. Keeping well away from the trigger, he put the gun on the floor and gave it a gentle push, it barely moved but the gesture was there.

'Who are you and what are you doing in our house?'

Trying to think on her feet Ruth said, 'We were fleeing Berlin, it's only a matter of time before the Russians get there, you can already hear the guns. We have family in Magdeburg.'

'Why isn't he in uniform?'

Ruth was just about to answer when he said, 'Can't he speak for himself?'

'No,' said Ruth, 'he was injured that's why he's not in uniform; he was honourably discharged just over a year ago.'

'Sit down,' he pointed the pistol at the chairs on the other side of the table, 'over there, and don't do anything stupid.'

Still with their hands raised Ruth and Ernie backed away behind the table and sat down, making sure they kept their hands in full view of the nervous man. He turned to the elderly woman.

'Mother, get the gun,' she scurried past him, still looking at them; she leant down and picked up the machine gun. Cautiously she backed away and gave her son the weapon. He unloaded it with obvious military training skills and placed it on a cupboard to his right.

'I'm surprised you aren't in uniform yourself the way you handled that gun,' said Ruth trying to keep some form of conversation going. The words hit a sore note; again he raised the pistol and pointed it at Ruth.

'DID I ASK YOU TO SPEAK?' Ruth dropped her head. What they did not know was that Johann Meier was a deserter. Only a week before he had turned up at the family farm just like Ernie and Ruth, cold, hungry and tired, begging his mother's forgiveness for deserting his post. At first she had told him he must go back, but now it appeared all was lost and it was just a matter of weeks, even days, before the war was over; what was the point? He would either be taken by the Allies as a POW, killed in the last throws of war, or shot for deserting. The odds were stacked so heavily against him she decided it was best he hid out there till it was all over. They had turned a small room into a secret compartment at the back of the house. So, when any patrols or authorities came by he could hide and she would say, as far as she knows he is fighting for the Fatherland, lay on a few tears, say how she missed her beloved son and that was that.

Calming himself a little Meier said, 'Why didn't you just try knocking the door instead of stealing from us?'

'We haven't exactly found people very welcoming these last few days, another minute or so and we would have been on our way. You wouldn't have even known we had been here except for a little missing bread and cheese,' said Ruth trying to reinforce the fact that it was only hunger that made them enter without permission, and there was no other ulterior motive.

'I was aware of you both before you even got to the wall, you were lucky I didn't shoot you then.'

Johann turned to his mother, 'Cut them a little bread and cheese.' He turned back to Ernie and Ruth, 'We can't spare much but we will share a little with you.' The woman cut two pieces of bread, then she sliced two decent wedges of cheese and slid them across the table.

'Thank you,' said Ruth, Ernie nodded his head and they both tucked into the food as if it was their last meal. They had just finished eating when the sound of a truck engine caught all their attention. Johann looked at his mother. He quickly dashed into the next room and in the darkness he peered through the window. Coming down the drive was Kohl's staff car, closely followed by the lorry loaded with troops. He ran back into the kitchen, 'We have to move quickly, there is a patrol.' Ruth and Ernie jumped to their feet. 'Follow me,' said Johann, 'there is a place we can hide.'

Ruth looked at Ernie who was obviously confused with everything that was going on. She took his arm and pulled him, Johann was already moving. As quickly as his legs would carry him he ran down the hall and turned left and up the stairs. Ernie grabbed the machine gun and magazine and he and Ruth quickly followed, his mother moving more slowly to watch them disappear along the landing.

Breathing deeply she composed herself, waiting for the inevitable knock on the door. Johann ran into the back bedroom, it all looked very normal. There was a chest of draws, bed, a large wardrobe, dressing table a few pictures on the walls; very ordinary. He went straight to the wardrobe, and opened the doors. It was full of dresses on coat hangers and a few pairs of shoes at the bottom. Ernie wondered what the hell was going on, were they all going to hide in a wardrobe? Was he mad? Johann separated the clothes and stepped in; part of the rear of the wardrobe had been removed. The wall the wardrobe had been placed against concealed a door. The wood of the door blended perfectly with the wood on the back of the wardrobe. You would never guess it was there. 'Quickly,' said Johann peering back at them from the room within. They followed him through the wardrobe and into the darkness. As soon as they were all in he pulled the wardrobe doors closed, straightened out the clothes hanging inside paired up the shoes so they didn't look as if they had been moved, then finally closed the door to the room.

'Sit down and be quiet.' Without saying a word Ruth pulled downwards on Ernie's arm. As they sat there in the darkness they both had the same train of thoughts. Why was he also hiding, had they missed something? Why did he look so rough, he needed a shave and his clothes looked filthy. Something wasn't quite right.

BANG BANG BANG, one of Kohl's men thumped the door hard with the palm of his hand. Kohl stood at the end of the path looking into the darkness. The elderly woman slowly made her way to the front door, trying to give her son as much time as possible to hide. She shouted out, 'Who's banging my door at this time of the evening?' She opened the door just enough to peer through the crack.

'Good evening,' said the soldier looking down at the eye peeping through the gap. 'We have reason to believe there are enemy agents in this area.' Kohl suddenly stepped up behind him.

'I will take it from here.'

'Yes sir,' said the soldier, stepping to one side to allow Kohl to pass.

'Good evening,' his fake smile was as transparent as the kitchen window. 'We are here to check on your safety, could we come in?

It won't take more than a few minutes of your time.' She contemplated what Kohl had said. Kohl was just about to kick the door in when she pulled it open; another second and his softly softly approach would have gone out of the window. Kohl smiled. 'Thank you Frau,' he hesitated waiting for her to introduce herself.

'Frau Meier,' she said, 'Winifred Meier, my husband was killed fighting in France and my son Johann is still fighting as far as I know'.

'I am very sorry for your loss, you must be very proud of your husband and son; I hope your son comes home safe soon.' All the time he was talking, Kohl scanned his surrounding looking for any sign of more than one inhabitant, but there was nothing. Kohl stepped past her and looked into the first room on his left, 'Have you seen anybody today?' The old lady took a deep breath and shook her head, 'Not for about a week, and that was a local farmer dropping off a few supplies, some locals have helped me since my son was called up.'

'I like that,' said Kohl, 'good German citizens pulling together during these hard times,' he glanced around the room. 'Then you won't mind if we have a quick look around, for your safety of course?'

'Not at all, Herr,' she hesitated just as Kohl had done waiting for his overdue introduction.

'My apologies, Herr Kohl, Gestapo.' He clipped his heals together and bowed his head a little.

'You men,' he called down the hall, 'four men search the house.' The troopers double timed up the path. Two went upstairs and two went straight through towards the kitchen.

Ernie's audience had depleted considerably. Alex was as engrossed as ever and his story had done wonders for his poppy sales.

'It was very clever what the man and his mother had done,' said Ernie, visualising the room. 'There was a window on our right hand side, so it wasn't totally pitch black, you could still just about make out each other's faces. If they had counted the windows on the front of the house, they would have realised there was a room they hadn't searched. Luckily they weren't that observant; it was all going well till I opened my big mouth.'

The soldiers began searching the house; they looked in every nook and cranny but gave the woman's belongings the respect they deserved. Ernie, Ruth and Johann sat on the floor in silence. Their ears reaching out for the slightest noise. As one of the soldiers came down the hall the sound of his boots on the floor boards sharpened their senses even more. They imagined him kneeling down to look under the bed. Then as he opened the wardrobe door, as one they felt their stomachs drop. They could hear the clothes moving on the rail as he checked inside. Had he realised there was a door behind it? All they could do was remain still and quiet. The wardrobe doors closed and the footsteps became more distant as he moved on through the house. They all breathed a sigh of relief.

Kohl was in the kitchen, still scanning for signs of cohabitation but could see nothing. A minute or two later the soldiers came in, 'All clear sir,' said one coming to attention.

'Very good,' said Kohl, 'wait outside and I will be there shortly,' he turned to the old lady, 'We won't take up another minute of your time, thank you for being so cooperative.' With that he turned and walked out of the kitchen door.

The soldiers had formed up outside and Kohl walked over to them as if he was about to inspect a parade. He glanced the first couple up and down, then stopped and said, 'We need to spread out in a straight line over an area of about one hundred yards,' he raised his hand and pointed across the field. 'Hauptmann Fleischer and the rest of the men will be coming from that direction. They can't be far away now. Remember the people we are searching for are armed and by now desperate, let's go.'

The men spread out in a line covering a good 100 yards. Weapons at the ready they started walking. Kohl left his driver with the staff car and truck.

Still sitting in silence Ernie was getting restless, unable to stay quiet any longer he said, 'I think they are gone.' In the darkness he reattached the magazine to the machine gun. When Ernie spoke the look on Johann's face was one of shock and horror; the thought that he had helped the enemy. He may have been a deserter, but he was a German through and through. Without warning he scurried back along the floor stood up and pulled out his pistol. Again with both hands squeezing the weapon a little too tightly for comfort he said, 'Put the weapon down.' Ruth immediately tried to discharge the situation by raising her hands and saying, 'Please, please, I can explain.'

'You don't need to explain anything,' said Johann, 'you are English spies.' The situation was tense; Ernie didn't want to give up the weapon again. The German's hands were shaking; the gun could go off any moment.

'Ernie, please,' said Ruth, 'put the gun down or he will shoot.' Ernie thought about it, he had to cock the weapon and point it at him, there was no way he would do that before the German got a couple of rounds off. Accepting defeat for now at least, Ernie slowly placed the machine gun on the floor in front of him then raised his hands submissively, hoping the German would calm down.

'Look,' said Ruth, 'we will be straight with you. I am a nurse, and yes he is English; but he's not a spy. He is a prisoner of war, and if I'm right he's just like you; he wants to be home with his family. We don't want any trouble, just to be on our way.' Ernie didn't know what Ruth had said, but even in the darkness he saw a change to the German's body language, whatever it was had hit home.

From previous situations they had been in, Ernie knew that Ruth was able to read situations and handle them diplomatically. Keeping a safe distance from them Johann said, 'Open the door.' Ruth pulled it open; as the light streamed in they half closed their eyes. Ernie knew the German patrol wasn't far away, but one way or another the situation had to be dealt with and soon. Ruth stepped through the back of the wardrobe first, closely followed by Ernie. Johann left the machine gun on the floor and followed holding out the Lugar in front of him. As Ernie stepped through the clothes for a brief second they closed together behind him. Johann's extended arm came through the clothes, gun pointing straight ahead, less than half a second before his torso. Ernie saw his chance; with every ounce of power he hit the man's wrist, knocking the gun from his hand. By some miracle the weapon didn't go off, Ernie grabbed him by the throat and sent him flying across the room. The man's momentum sent him straight over the dressing table and he crashed to the floor in a heap. Rather than go for the pistol Ernie leapt on Johann's chest and starting raining punches into his head from every angle. The German tried to resist but it was futile, he was no match for Ernie's combat experience. Without remorse Ernie hit him again and again, his face was a bloody mess, his nose disintegrated with two or three sickening cracks.

'STOP,' shouted Ruth, 'STOP ERNIE!' Johann could barely breathe, his facial features totally destroyed. Ruth was trembling; she had never seen such rage between one human being and another. She had only ever seen the gentle side of Ernie, she saw the aftermath in the forest earlier that day but to experience it first-hand really frightened her. Ernie climbed off his chest and quickly made his way over to the discarded pistol. Adrenalin still coursing through his body Ernie looked at Ruth, 'Quickly fetch the machine gun I'll keep an eye on him.' Without question Ruth stepped back through the wardrobe and retrieved the machine gun. Ernie said to the German, 'I didn't want to do that fella, but you left me no option.' Ruth gave the machine gun to Ernie then said in German, 'He apologises for hitting you, we just wanted to be on our way.'

'Ask him about the motorbike,' said Ernie tidying himself up and wiping the man's blood from his knuckles, 'ask him if it still runs.'

Once more acting as an interpreter Ruth turned back to Johann, who had now sat himself up and was leaning against the bedroom wall, blood freely flowing from his nose and mouth.

Johann, barely able to lift his own head up glanced at Ernie then back to Ruth, struggling to talk he said, 'It's temperamental to start,' his breathing was shallow and hindered, 'but once it's going its fine,' he stopped for a moment, 'half a dozen kicks and you will be away and good riddance.'

Ruth turned back to Ernie, 'Yes it works,' after seeing what Ernie was capable of she didn't want to tell him exactly what the German had said in case he struck him again. As Ernie stared at the German he said, 'Tell him not to move from this room till he hears that motorbike disappear into the distance. If I see him again, I will kill him - that's a promise, tell him that word for word.'

Whether he meant it or was just trying to frighten him, it frightened Ruth. She repeated his statement word for word. Johann gave no response, he just sat in his own blood, content for now with still being alive.

Ernie stared at the German as he cocked the machine gun. It was a kind of warning, he still gave no response, he just leaned against the wall and pinched what was left of his nose with his thumb and index finger. Ruth was in front of Ernie, placing his hand on her shoulder he said, 'Let me go first down the stairs, stay close to me.' She didn't need telling twice, Ernie pulled the Lugar from his belt and gave it to her, 'If you have to use it, don't hesitate,' Ernie stared straight into her eyes trying to emphasise the importance of what he had just said. She nodded in acknowledgement of his request, whether she could or not only time would tell. Slowly they went down the stairs, keeping their backs close to the wall. Ernie kept the barrel of the machine gun raised in front of him. As they got to the bottom the old lady came out of the kitchen and stood at the end of the hall.

Seeing Ernie with the machine gun and Ruth with the pistol she asked, 'Where is my son?'

'He's alright,' said Ruth, 'he's in the back bedroom, he agrees its best we leave quickly; now the patrol has gone.' She didn't know whether to believe them or not, but there was nothing she could do either way. She stood back to allow them passage. Ernie kept a firm grip on the machine gun as he walked past the obviously anxious woman. Ruth followed still staying very close to Ernie.

Opening the kitchen door Ernie peered out into the night, there was no sign of the German patrol. Again Ernie looked at Ruth, 'It all looks clear, once we get that bike going we are out of here.' The motorbike was leaning against a stone wall; he had seen this bike before but never without a side car. It was a BMW R75, and was made specifically for the military. His brothers had pictures of them at home; he remembered his brother Arthur saying it was a big heavy bike.

Without looking at Ruth he told her to wait while quickly he ran across the yard looking and listening all around him. He took the cap off the fuel tank and peered inside, he tapped the side of the tank looking for any movement; there was some fuel but not a lot, it would have to do. As long as it got them away from there. He put the cap back on and reached underneath, turning on the fuel tap. With the machine gun slung on his back he pulled the bike up straight and cocked his leg over. Straight away he felt the weight of the bike. Looking down he searched for the kickstart pedal. Once he found it he put his heel on it and mentally counted, one, two, three. With all his might he forced the pedal down. It turned over but didn't start. There was a switch in the middle of the handle bars above the tank. He remembered his brother telling him the electrics worked by something called a magneto; he flicked the switch on and tried again, still it didn't start.

On the other side of the farmhouse, unknown to Ernie and Ruth the staff car driver leaned against his vehicle smoking a cigarette. The sound of Ernie trying to kick start the bike caught his attention. He stood up, dropped his cigarette and ground it into the dirt with the heel of his boot. There was only an old lady in the farmhouse; the likelihood of it being her was very slim. He unclipped his sidearm and with his pistol drawn he cautiously worked his way round the edge of the building.

Ernie continued kicking the bike over again and again, working the throttle as he jumped on the pedal. Ernie said out loud, 'Come on you son of a',!!!Broom!!!, the engine burst into life, 'Yes,' said Ernie out loud. He looked back at Ruth and smiled just as the staff driver came round the corner. He saw Ernie but not Ruth; she was just inside the door out of his vision.

Holding the pistol out in front of him with both hands he shouted, 'Get off the bike or I will shoot.' Ernie never had a chance to pull the machine gun from his back. Ruth knew she was their only hope. Ernie's eyes moved from the German to Ruth in a split second. The staff driver picked up on it straight away and glanced in Ruth's direction. Ruth had already raised the pistol Ernie had given her. Almost in slow motion the German's gun started to change targets. She couldn't hesitate or they were both dead. He hadn't even got half way to his new target when Ruth opened fire. BANG BANG, two shots rang out, both hitting their target; one in his chest and the other in his stomach. His jaw dropped open as he looked down at the crimson fluid flowing from his chest and slowly the pistol fell from his hand. His eyes raised towards Ruth, as if to say 'Why me?' Then he dropped to his knees and fell flat on his face.

Hearing the gun shots in the distance, Kohl and his men came to an abrupt halt. Sounding so close behind them, they must have come from the farmhouse. Not too far in front of them, out of the darkness the silhouettes Hauptmann Fleischer and his men approached. Kohl raised his hand and shouted, 'Back to the farmhouse quickly,' Kohl's line of men turned and in double time ran back in the direction of the farmhouse. As Fleischer jogged up to Kohl, his men close on his shoulder Kohl said, 'I think we have found our fox.'

Ruth was still holding the gun out in front of her, pointing where the staff driver had been standing, her body frozen with the shock of what she had just done. All her training was about saving lives not taking them; of course it was exactly the opposite for Ernie. 'Ruth,' he shouted, 'come on, snap out of it, they will be here in seconds.' Ernie glanced over his shoulder; he could hear voices in the dark. 'Ruth, we have to go now. Suddenly something clicked in her head. Like waking from a dream she squinted her eyes and shook her head. Ernie was sat on the motorbike; it looked like he was shouting something but nothing was coming out of his mouth. Then the volume was suddenly turned to maximum, 'Ruth, we have to go.'

He gestured her over to him. She dropped the pistol and ran; straddling the rear of the bike and putting her arms around Ernie's waist.

'Hold tight,' said Ernie, she increased her grip. Ernie pushed the gear shift down and let out the clutch. The yard was very uneven, and Ernie struggled at first to keep the bike up straight, but the sound of boots and German voices helped him considerably. The back wheel skidded left then right out of nowhere, the sound of machine gun fire made them tuck their heads in as close as possible. The brick wall to their left exploded with a hail of stone chips, as the bullets ricocheted along its length. Ernie steered round the farmhouse past the lorry and up the dirt path road. Bullets flew all around them narrowly missing their heads. The motorbike powered up the hill onto the main round and off into the night. They weren't sure if they were going in the right direction, but for now, anywhere would do.

'Blimey that was close Ernie.'

'You're telling me,' said the old veteran, 'to this day I'm amazed Ruth didn't get one in the back, the bullets were bouncing off everything around us. I guess it was just our lucky day.'

With a broad smile on his face Alex said, 'You had a few of them by the sound of things.'

The old man smiled, 'I think they had been told to capture us rather than kill us, either that or they were pretty bad shots, even in the dark you would have thought one of them would have hit us. We just kept our heads down and hoped for the best. The bike served a purpose but it didn't last long.'

Alex sat up again anxious for the next part of the old man's story, 'Why?'

'Ran out of fuel,' said Ernie, 'We got about five miles down the road and it packed up.' 'Were they still after you?'

'Oh yes, I don't know what went on at that farmhouse after we escaped. But they really stepped up the chase.'

In the farmhouse Johann had made his way down the stairs. He sat at the kitchen table while his mother carefully cleaned up the wounds on his face. After Kohl's men reported back to him about the couple escaping on the motorbike, he was in no mood for messing about. Kohl and Fleischer walked round to the farmhouse kitchen door. Already two troopers were stood there waiting for their orders.

As Kohl approached he simply said, 'Kick it down,' the troopers followed his orders to the detail. The door was virtually off in seconds and, machine guns at the ready they stepped into the kitchen. At the top of his voice one shouted, 'ON YOUR FEET NOW, HANDS IN THE AIR,' Johann and his mother complied as quickly as they could. Kohl walked in followed by Fleischer who had to bow his head slightly under the door frame. Kohl went straight over to the old lady. She looked him straight in the eye, too long in the tooth to be intimidated by a man barely as tall as her. 'It appears Frau Meier you weren't telling me the truth.' His same old insincere smile indicating she was in serious trouble.

Johann suddenly spoke out, 'It wasn't,' WHACK; the butt of one of the trooper's weapons hit him just below the sternum. He dropped down to his knees between the table and his chair. As the pain seared through his torso he retched trying to breath and vomit all at the same time.

Kohl turned to the trooper that had dealt the blow, 'Thank you.'

As quickly as her body could move, the old lady got down on one knee to aid her son.

'Stand-up,' said Kohl aggressively. Together they struggled back to their feet, Johann still fighting to keep the contents of his stomach down. Kohl looked him up and down then said, 'I take it you would like to contribute to the conversation.' Johann was about to speak when Kohl raised a hand and stopped him, 'Before you do, please humour me. Who exactly are you?'

Johann swallowed hard and took a deep breath, 'My name is Johann Meier, I was discharged from active service on medical grounds just over two months ago.' Kohl rubbed his chin with his thumb and index finger, 'Uummh,' he thought for a moment then said, 'Apart from the obvious injuries to your face you don't look like a man that would have been discharged. Especially with the current situation at the front, there are grandfathers and young boys preparing to defend the Fatherland and you're telling me they sent you home?'

Kohl shook his head and walked around the room. He suddenly stopped turned and looked at them and said, 'Harbouring fugitives of the state is punishable by death.' Johann went to speak; the trooper again raised the butt of his weapon Johann flinched and raised his hands in defence.

Kohl raised his hand to stop the soldier delivering another painful blow. 'You were about to say,' said Kohl.

'They held me hostage upstairs in the bedroom; they told my mother they would kill me if she said anything. Please, sir, we are a good German family.' Again Kohl thought for a moment. 'Feasible, I suppose.'

Johann interrupted him again, 'They burst in, took me by surprise.' Johann held his hand up to his nose, 'This is what they did to me for resisting.' Kohl bought the story, how else would he have got into such a state?

'That still does not explain why you are not in active service.'

'I told you, I was discharged.' Kohl smiled, he wasn't buying that part of the story.

'I take it that was your bike they used to escape on?'

'Yes sir, but they won't get far, the tank was almost empty.'

Kohl smiled, 'That my friend is the first good thing you have said to me.' Johann smiled painfully back thinking he was winning him over. Kohl turned to the soldier next to him, 'Take him outside and shoot him for desertion.' Johann's face dropped, 'But sir, we are good German people!' The soldier stared at Kohl dumbfounded with what he had just been told to do. A few seconds later Kohl now biting his top lip as his temper grew, turned back to the soldier, 'Are you deaf?'

'No sir,' said the soldier coming to attention.

'Well get on with it.' They pulled the table to one side and two soldiers grabbed Johann, one under each arm. With his mother frantically pulling at one of their shoulders, they dragged him across the room and past the remnants of what was once the kitchen door and out into the yard.

During Kohl's exchange of words, Hauptmann Fleischer had stood on the other side of the room dissecting everything that had been said. He felt sure the man had been held hostage, and he probably was a deserter. However, under the circumstances, he should have arrested him and gone through the correct procedure. Once found guilty he probably would have been shot, but that wasn't their decision.

Kohl turned to Fleischer, 'I think we could still catch them before morning if we move immediately.' Fleischer couldn't believe the callousness of the man, ruthless was an understatement. 'Where were you dragged up Kohl?' asked Fleischer with a familiar look of distaste on his face. Kohl looked surprised.

'I beg your pardon?' responded Kohl surprised by Fleischer's renewed verbal abuse.

'Well you can't possibly come from a normal family upbringing.'
'Actually my father was hugely significant in the rise to power of our much loved Führer. What I would call a pillar of political society.' That explains a lot, thought Fleischer.

'What about your mother?' asked Fleischer.

'Unfortunately she died when I was very young, a political reprisal my father claims, he dealt with those in question.'

'It didn't help your mother though did it?' said Fleischer. He could see now that Kohl's whole life had been nothing more than a constant power struggle. It was his attempt at reproducing, or even bettering, his father's influence on society.

'BANG,' from outside the farmhouse a single shot rang out. Fleischer felt his heart drop, just a little.

'I pity you,' he said to Kohl. From the yard Johann's mother could be heard screaming and sobbing. Her son lay flat on his back, a single bullet hole in the side of his head. A crimson fountain pulsed from the perfectly round hole. His mother pressed the palm of her hand over the wound, in some way thinking he could still be saved, but it wasn't to be. As the blood covered her hands the rage built up inside her. Even at her age the maternal instinct was as strong as ever. Leaning against the fence was a two pronged pitchfork. The soldier who fired the shot was walking away holstering his sidearm. With remarkable speed for someone of such age, she leapt to her feet and grabbed the pitchfork. The only thing on her mind now was to kill the man that executed her son. As he walked away she ran at his back, her intention to drive the pitch fork deep into him. Ten feet, six feet, three feet, BANG, the soldier flinched at the gun shot and turned all at the same time. He would not have avoided the thrust of the fork. Stood in the doorway with his pistol at arm's length, Kohl had seen everything. Before she could deliver what would have been a fatal thrust, Kohl had fired a single shot hitting her in the centre of the chest. She was probably dead before she hit the floor. The soldier looked at Kohl and came to attention.

'Thank you sir.'

Kohl pushed his pistol into his pocket and said 'It's the live ones you must not take your eyes off soldier, not the dead ones.' The soldier lowered his head more in embarrassment than the shock of the incident.

'Let's go, we have a fox to catch.' shouted Kohl. He pointed at the soldier he had just saved from certain death.

'You are now my driver.'

'Yes sir,' came a relieved reply. The men in double time climbed into the back of the truck. Fleischer, again unable to speak to Kohl after what he had just witnessed, got into the front of the truck. As they drove off in the direction the bike was last seen, the aftermath of yet another one of Kohl's war crimes lay in silence. No witnesses or clues as to what had happened there, no one to answer to except themselves.

'So without transport what did you do?' asked Alex, 'They can't have been that far behind you and you had killed another one of their men. They must have been more than a little pissed off with you by now, if you'll excuse my French.'

'Well, we had no choice; we had to go cross country. It was our only option, and to top it off I picked up another injury.' Five miles from the farmhouse, Ernie and Ruth stood at the side of the road. The sound of distant shelling seemed to be getting louder.

'That's it,' said Ernie, 'we're on foot again, the fuel tank's empty.' They looked all around them, in the distance the sky seemed to glow.

'That must be what's left of Magdeburg,' said Ruth. 'Looks like it's taking one hell of a pounding, remember what Leon from the forest people said? Avoid it.'

'I think he was right,' said Ernie shaking his head slightly at the sight before him. 'If we can go slightly south we might just avoid what's left of the German army.' Ruth nodded her head in agreement.

'I think from memory there is a lot of forestry south of Magdeburg before the river. Not sure how far but it's probably the safest way with them trailing us.'

'Sounds like a good plan,' said Ernie, 'that chap back at the farmhouse will be singing like a canary after the beating I gave him. Let's push the bike off the road and try to throw them off our scent.'

They pushed the bike down the small embankment at the side of the road and let it go. It rolled about ten yards on its own then the front wheel disappeared down a hole. The back end of the bike, as heavy as it was, suddenly raised in the air, almost vertically like a monument in the middle of a field.

'Jesus Christ,' said Ernie, 'Why don't we just put a sign on the road saying "turn left"?' Ernie ran over to the bike, he was no more than a couple of yards away when he fell. His right leg found a pot hole about eighteen inches deep, just big enough for his foot, 'crack.' He screamed out in pain as he fell to the floor. Cautiously in the darkness, Ruth made her way over to him, now being very careful of the terrain.

'I think it's broken,' said Ernie through gritted teeth. 'I heard one hell of a crack as my foot went down the hole.' Ruth very carefully took hold of his ankle. Thankfully there was no sign of any open fracture or obvious deformity to his lower leg or ankle. With both hands holding his foot she moved it slightly to one side, 'Arrrgh,' cried out Ernie in pain. 'It's no good girl, you are going to have to leave me.'

Ruth gave him a look of disbelief, 'Are you mad?'

'Well I don't think I can walk.'

'With me under your arm you will, come on get up.'

Once again Ruth was showing a whole new side to her character. Hearing the determination in her voice, Ernie gritted his teeth and with every ounce of energy and Ruth's assistance; he pulled himself to his feet. Breathing hard, with Ernie mentally overcoming the pain, they set off. Keeping the glow of Magdeburg ahead to their right, some way off in the distance was the comforting edge of what they hoped was the start of a dense forest, which would give them the invisibility they now required.

Kohl, Fleischer and the patrol continued along the road directly outside the farm. There was no other way they could have gone. Kohl told his new driver to keep his speed down and keep his eyes peeled for any lanes or tracks off the main road the bike could have taken. The sound of heavy shelling and the glow in the sky had the men on edge. Still, Kohl pressed on.

Ernie and Ruth had thirty minutes head start, but as they were now on foot and Ernie was injured, this amounted to nothing. If they could just make it to the forest, they had a chance. Fifteen minutes passed and still no sign; Kohl was starting to doubt whether he was going to catch them. The soldier at the back of the truck looked out into the night. Someway off the road to his right he spotted what appeared to be a wheel sticking up in the air.

It was a bike. 'Stop the truck!' he shouted at the top of his voice, startling the other men. One of the men at the front banged on the rear of the cab, 'Stop!' Fleischer, whose eyes were becoming a little heavy, suddenly jumped up in his seat, 'Pull over and flash your lights.' The driver did as he was told; Kohl's driver saw the lights flashing in his mirror.

'Sir, they are flashing their lights at us.'

'Pull over,' said Kohl. Kohl looked out of the back window, 'reverse back let's see what's wrong.' Fleischer was already out of the cab and round the back when Kohl got there.

'About fifty yards back sir,' said the soldier, 'It looked like a bike wheel sticking up in the air.'

'Four men,' said Fleischer, 'Out the truck, go and investigate.' Four soldiers including the one that spotted it jumped down over the back board and ran down the road.

With torches on, they scanned the area, and it didn't take long to find. 'HERE SIR!' shouted one of the soldiers. Kohl and Fleischer went down to where the soldiers had left the road. They were stood next to the bike, looking very pleased with themselves.

'Good job, men,' called out Fleischer as he stepped off the road. Fleischer looked out into the darkness. He thought to himself: if that was me what would I do? They are no fools, they have evaded us once too often.

Seeing the glow in the sky that was obviously a no go area unless you were reinforcing the German front line, he looked slightly left, 'The forest south of Magdeburg, that is where they are heading. We have till first light, once they are in the forest we won't find them. We haven't got the manpower to search such dense woodland.' Kohl said nothing; Fleischer obviously knew the area better than him. 'I will take the same number of men as before with me cross country and try to catch them up,' he turned round and looked at Kohl, 'You take the rest, make sure you get to the tree line before light, spread out and wait for us. It's quite a way as you have to follow the road straight ahead for some distance. Then turn sharp left at a T junction and it comes back to the forest.' Without hesitation Kohl nodded in agreement, his reputation for always getting his man was being tested to the limit.

'Let's go,' shouted Kohl, 'we have no time to waste.'

Once again the men split up and some climbed into the back of the truck; others climbed out and rallied on Fleischer, awaiting their orders. As the vehicles disappeared into the night, Fleischer, with his men out in a long line and with a new level of determination, set off on foot, torches on and weapons at the ready. The next couple of hours would determine the outcome of their mission one way or another.

'Was it broken Ernie?' asked Alex waiting for the old man to reveal the next part of his story.

'No, but it felt like it, I just had to grit my teeth and get on with it. My old girl came up trumps again. We hadn't been moving long when she told me to take my jacket off. Well you can imagine it was cold,' the old man had a little chuckle to himself. 'The look I gave her, she said "don't argue just do it." As soon as I got my jacket off she grabbed my shirt and ripped the bloomin sleeve off.'

Alex laughed, 'You're joking.'

'I'm not, and then she goes "sit down"; well I sat down on a rock and she pulled me boot off. I nearly jumped in the air it was so painful. She wrapped up my ankle so tight I couldn't have moved it if I'd wanted to, but it did the job, took my weight and doubled my speed.'

'She was some woman your Ruth.'

'She was that,' said Ernie, reminiscing. 'After everything I've told you we had been through, what happened next was probably the most amazing piece of luck anyone could have had.' Alex again sat up straight; Ernie thought for moment then took a deep breath. 'We made it to the forest by the skin of our teeth, but we weren't the only ones that did.'

Ernie and Ruth pushed on into the night, tired was an understatement, they were both out on their feet. Some way off behind them they could see what looked like the occasional cigarette end in the dark. Ernie had a good idea it was the glow of distant soldiers' torches, but didn't want to worry his already frightened heroine. He was moving well; at this rate they would reach the forest before the patrol caught up with them. Seeing signs of daylight on the horizon quickened their pace. Unfortunately, it also quickened the pace of the patrol. Kohl on the other hand wasn't having much luck. A couple of miles down the road what looked like parts of an armoured vehicle were blocking the route. In the darkness Kohl's driver saw them at the last moment and managed to swerve and miss. The truck wasn't so lucky; the right hand front wing collided with a couple of ton of tracks and tank armour bringing the vehicle to an abrupt halt. The men in the back of the truck were shook up but not injured. It was easily fixable, but the time to do it was a commodity Kohl didn't have.

'Keep going girl,' said Ernie as he glanced over his shoulder, not wanting to alarm Ruth but at the same time keeping a close eye on what he suspected was the pursuing patrol. It would be light in another half an hour or so. The tree line loomed in front of them; safety was so close. Ernie was now moving quite well on his damaged ankle. It was Ruth that was struggling; sheer exhaustion was starting to get the better of her. Less than a mile away Kohl and the rest of the patrol raced down the tree line. They had lost a lot of time repairing the truck, he just hoped he hadn't missed them; the word failure was not in his vocabulary. Kohl sat up in his staff car, hands perched on the back of the driver's seat.

'Pull over,' he said, anxiously, 'As the crow flies this is approximately where they should enter the forest.' Unknown to him, he was a good quarter of a mile short.

Ernie and Ruth heard the vehicles before they saw them. Fortunately the landscape was very uneven and there were plenty of mounds of dirt and bushes to hide behind. All the same, they had to make a break for the tree line before it was completely light. They were so close they could hear orders being shouted. Kohl had got the door of his car open before his driver could get out,

'Quickly,' shouted Kohl. 'Spread out in a line down the road.' The soldiers leapt from the back of the truck and started jogging down the road, spreading out as they went. Ernie knew this was it; they had to go for it, even if they were seen. Once the soldiers were in front of them on the road they were trapped. Ernie looked at Ruth, 'We've got to make a run for it.' She stared back at him, fear in her eyes. 'Stay low and keep to my left, when I say run do just that and don't look back; just keep going. You got that?' Ruth nodded, her breathing already sounded laboured, more from fear than exhaustion. Ernie checked the machine gun, thinking, 'safety catch off one up the spout.' Bent double they started moving, their eyes fixed firmly on the soldiers on the road. Another 150 yards they would be in the forest and in with a chance. As quickly as they could in such an uncomfortable posture, they half ran half crawled. Ernie realised for the last thirty or forty yards they would be in the open, no cover whatsoever from bushes or mounds of earth. Reaching out with his left hand still focusing on the soldiers he grabbed Ruth's arm.

'Keep close alongside me now girl,' If he had to put himself between the soldiers' bullets and Ruth, so be it. He knew it was just a matter of time before they were spotted. Just before the open land Ernie stopped.

Chapter 23

'This is it,' said Ernie looking straight into Ruth's eyes. 'Once we start running now, don't stop for anything, you got that?'

'But what if?'

'Nothing, do you hear me?' He put the back of his hand on her cheek and smiled, 'We can do this.'

She gave a slight knowing nod, raised her hand and held his. 'I love you Ernie White,'

'Likewise,' replied Ernie, 'Let's go.' They set off, upright and running as fast as their legs would carry them. It looked as if it was going well; they were going to make it, and unseen.

Suddenly, 'HALT!' shouted a German voice. They paid no attention just kept running, the sound of machine gun fire roared out, their bodies contracted as if they were trying to make themselves smaller. Ernie looked to his right; only thirty yards away a German soldier stood pointing his machine gun in the air. The first shots were obviously to stop them in their tracks. They must have been told to take them alive if possible. He knew from experience the next volley would be aimed at them, probably low a wounding shot to bring them down.

As he ran he aimed his machine gun in the general direction of the soldier and fired off a few rounds. Although Ernie didn't see it, as he was more concerned with escaping than taking them on, the soldier fell to his knees then rolled onto his side clutching at his stomach. Hearing the soldier shout and fire, his comrades further down the road ran in his direction.

'CRACK,' Ernie ducked as a bullet went straight over his head, much too close for comfort. It was Fleischer and his men moving at an alarming speed in the open land right behind them. As they entered the tree line bullets ricocheted off the surrounding trees and branches. They obviously had no problem with killing them, given the chance.

'Keep going,' said Ernie, glancing over his shoulder. Once Ruth was a good few yards in front of him he stopped and turned. Dropping onto one knee he opened fire. Being in dense undergrowth he couldn't see his targets but it had the desired effect. With bullets flying all around them and unable to see where they were coming from, the advancing patrol went to ground. Ernie quickly emptied the magazine. Having no more ammunition he threw down the machine gun, stood up and ran in Ruth's direction.

Fleischer was already back on his feet and moving forward. The rest of the patrol did not move. Now a good few yards in front of his men he stopped and turned. 'Come on, get up, let's go.' The soldier closest to him said, 'He's reloading sir.'

'Nonsense' said Fleischer, 'he's out of ammunition.' Then from the tree directly in front of them shots rang out, 'CRACK, CRACK, CRACK.' More by luck than judgement one went straight over Fleischer's head, he dropped straight down to the floor. The soldier looked at him and raised his eyebrows, as if to say 'I told you so.' Ruth had seen Ernie stop and discharge his weapon. As he caught up with her she fired off three rounds from the hand gun he had given her. Realising there were no bullets left she threw the pistol in their direction and they both gave flight, trying to find the fastest and quietest way through the dense woodland.

Fleischer was now up again and on one knee. Still convinced they were virtually, if not completely, out of ammunition he waited thirty seconds then got back to his feet. He pointed his pistol at the soldier that had opposed him and said, 'Get up now or I will shoot you for insubordination.' The rest of the men looked dumb struck, 'And that applies to the rest of you also.' It worked and they quickly got to their feet, cautiously moving towards the tree line. As they reached the trees Kohl came down the road moving more quickly than Fleischer had ever seen. Fleischer holstered his pistol.

'Hauptmann Fleischer, I have sent the rest of the men into the forest further down the road. They won't get far. We will flank them, your men can mop up what's left of them from the rear.' Fleischer looked up into the sky and took a handkerchief from his pocket. As he wiped the sweat from his brow he said, 'I told you, if they make the trees they are gone, it will be like looking for a needle in a haystack with this number of men.'

'We are so close,' said Kohl, 'they are only minutes in front of us.'

Fleischer shook his head, he had to give it to him, he was persistent. 'Noon,' said Fleischer, 'then we call it off.'

'Deal,' said Kohl.

Fleischer again drew his side arm, waved it in the air in the direction of the forest and shouted, 'Spread out, stay alert, let's finish this.' Leading his men, Fleischer entered the forest. Ten yards back, cautious as ever, Kohl, ensuring he wasn't in any danger, brought up the rear.

'That's what you call lucky.' said Alex, amazed at what the veteran had just considered good fortune. Ernie raised his head and made eye contact.

'I'm still here aren't I?'

Alex thought about it, 'Well yes but...'

'But nothing,' interjected Ernie. 'Only God knows how we got through that hail of bullets as we went into the trees. I had a badly sprained ankle, but there was so much adrenalin running through my body I never felt a thing till later. Anyway that wasn't the piece of luck I was referring to.' 'You mean you had more good fortune?' asked Alex with a broad smile on his face.

'We sure did, you see they didn't stop there, they came into the forest after us.'

Both gasping for breath after running flat out for a good fifteen minutes, Ernie and Ruth stopped. Trying to keep a low profile they went down onto one knee. Ernie quickly scanned all around them, they could have been running round in circles, everything looked the same. If he had a compass it would have been a different situation, but he didn't.

'I think we should go to ground,' said Ernie still cautiously surveying the surrounding trees and undergrowth.

'What do you mean?' asked Ruth a little confused.

'If we are going round in circles eventually we are going to walk straight into that patrol.' Ruth looked worried, Ernie took her hand, 'You trust me don't you?'

Ruth nodded, 'Of course.'

The trees around them were covered in tangle weed. 'We haven't got long so listen. Quickly and quietly wrap as much of this tangle weed,' he tore some off a nearby branch and showed it to her, 'around your arms, legs and body, got that?' Ruth quickly nodded and went to work; Ernie did the same and within a couple of minutes they were both covered in it. Ernie stuck three fingers in the dirt and ran his fingers over Ruth's face, producing streaks of camouflage. He did the same to himself then he looked into her eyes, laughed and said, 'Very attractive.' Some yards away, just before a clearing, a large tree had fallen down. The tangle weed had grown all over it, across the ground and up the surrounding trees. 'That will do nicely,' said Ernie, The trunk of the tree was riddled with holes and the weed virtually covered it on the forest floor.

'Get under there,' Ruth did as he asked, it wasn't pleasant. Damp fungal growths covered the floor under the weed. Trying not to disrupt the natural growth patterns Ernie covered her up. Once he was happy, he crawled under and positioned the weeds around himself the best he could. As Ernie lay on his side he looked at Ruth and quietly said, 'It could be some time before they give up the chase, no matter what happens stay perfectly still and they'll walk straight past.'

Not keen on the idea, but not really having much option Ruth nodded her head just slightly, 'Whatever you say.'

Fleischer and his men advanced into the forest, Kohl sent one of the men back down the road to catch up with the rest of the patrol and inform the NCO in charge exactly what they planned to do. The idea was good, but in such dense forestry, virtually impossible. But Kohl was adamant, so that was that. The deeper they went into the forest, even though it was only mid-morning, the gloom and at times almost darkness made it feel like late evening. After nearly an hour, unknown to them, they had already passed their prey tucked away under the fallen tree. Suddenly in front of them was movement. Almost completely synchronised all the patrol dropped onto one knee. Weapons pointing at the rustling undergrowth; from out of the trees came the remainder of the patrol. 'Woo,' said the soldier at the front raising his hands in the air, 'Steady where you're pointing those weapons.' The men lowered their guns; Fleischer turned to Kohl who was still a good distance behind them. 'That's it then,' said Fleischer, 'They're gone.' Kohl said nothing. For a brief second he stared at Fleischer then turned and started walking in the direction they had come from. Fleischer thought for a moment, if the escapees had continued running, surely there would have at least been signs in the undergrowth, damaged branches and so on. The penny dropped: they had gone to ground, they had anticipated what Kohl was trying to do.

'Herr Kohl,' Fleischer called out, Kohl stopped and turned. 'I have a theory. I think they are hiding in the undergrowth somewhere between here and the road. I haven't seen one broken branch or footprint for nearly an hour. When we first started through the forest it was pretty obvious which way they went.'

Kohl almost smiled, 'So how do we flush them out?'

'We don't,' said Fleischer. 'We go back the way we came. Make them believe we have given up, but we leave four men here with orders not to move for fifteen minutes. Then slowly and quietly they follow in our footsteps, they might just make a run for it a little while after we have passed them.'

'If you're right Hauptmann Fleischer, it could work.'

'Have you any better ideas?' The trap was set. Fleischer handpicked the four men including two experienced NCO's. The other soldiers set off back through the forest unaware of their superiors' plans.

Sometime later Ernie and Ruth were lying as still as humanly possible. Not too far away they heard the sound of branches breaking as the patrol came back in their direction. Sluggishly they walked through the trees, their enthusiasm to complete the mission now gone.

Ernie whispered to Ruth, 'Stay still and quiet.' One by one the patrol passed their position, at times unnervingly close. As they disappeared into the undergrowth Ernie took a deep breath, quietly he whispered, 'Just a little longer, then we will make a move.' Ruth didn't reply, the whole experience for her had been traumatising. Five minutes passed then ten; Ernie could see Ruth shivering with the cold. They hadn't moved for well over two hours. This deep in the forest there was very little sunlight and the ground was damp.

'We'll back up now,' said Ernie, 'but keep down and keep the camouflage on you till I say different, got it?' Ruth nodded relieved they were finally on the move again, slowly together they moved backwards from the weed covered tree trunk, 'CLICK.' It was a sound Ernie knew only too well, the release of a safety catch. A German soldier stood directly behind them, machine gun at the ready. 'Stand up, keep your hands where I can see them.' Ernie glanced at Ruth unable to understand the words, but knowing the meaning of the soldiers command, slowly they got up. Their bodies were now so cold that if the opportunity to disarm the soldier presented itself, they probably couldn't have reacted in time. 'Over here,' shouted the soldier. Within seconds three more soldiers appeared from the surrounding trees. One, obviously their superior, walked over to Ernie. Standing face to face with him, he grinned, deliberately intimidating Ernie. 'You have lead us a merry chase my friend.'

Ernie turned to Ruth for some idea as to what he had said when suddenly, THUMP, the butt of the soldier's weapon hit him just below the sternum. Ernie fell to his knees in agony, unable to take a breath. Ruth exploded in anger at Ernie's treatment. In German she shouted, 'What did you do that for you filthy scum?' She was unable to say another word; the butt of the weapon hit her straight on the point of her jaw and, she blacked out. Although in a great deal of pain Ernie saw red. He lunged forward, rugby tackling the soldier to the ground. He scrambled up the soldier's legs, fists ready to destroy his assailant. THUMP, a rifle butt hit him square on the temple, and he passed out.

Ernie woke with a start as a sudden deluge of water cascaded over his face. He tried to take a deep breath but his mouth was half full of water. Ingesting more than his body could cope with he rolled onto his side coughing and spluttering. As he lay on his side wondering what the hell had happened, he saw Ruth kneeling down and sobbing uncontrollably. It all came rushing back to him; hiding in the undergrowth, the patrol walking past them. Yes, the lone soldier sneaking up behind them, they had fallen for the oldest trick in the book. Ernie tried to sit up but the pain in his stomach and chest still hadn't subsided. They were in a clearing surrounded by trees and all about them were armed German soldiers, under his breath he said, 'Shit.'

Two soldiers grabbed him under the armpits and pulled him to his feet. Fleischer walked over, towering above him, in English said, 'You have caused us a lot of grief and embarrassment, Englishman.'

Ernie looked up at him and, with more than a hint of sarcasm replied, 'I'm so sorry I'll try and do a better job next time.' Ernie turned to Ruth and smiled as if to say, 'Stuff them.'

Fleischer, enraged by Ernie's arrogance, suddenly and unexpectedly punched him in the gut. Still in pain from the previous assault, Ernie collapsed to his knees and leaned against the German officer's legs. Fleischer took a step back, and before Ernie hit the floor the officer's over size boot hit him square in the ribs. Ruth who was being restrained by one of the soldiers screamed out loud, 'Stop it!' Pulling herself free from the soldier's grips she ran forward dropping on top of Ernie, trying to protect him from any more abuse. Kohl stepped forward. He had derived some kind of sadistic pleasure watching Fleischer take his anger out on their prisoner. Now it was his turn, 'You two,' pointing at the nearest two soldiers, 'Get her off him.' As they stepped forward Kohl said, 'You my dear can ride in the back of the truck with the men, it has been a while since they have had the pleasure of a woman. I am sure they will find something to do with you. As for him, stick him in the,' 'BANG,' a fountain of crimson spurted from the side of Kohl's head.

He fell forward, landing right on top of Ruth and Ernie. From that moment all hell let loose, as the German soldiers raised their weapons to an unseen enemy. One by one they were cut down. From the surrounding trees all that could be seen were muzzle flashes. The Germans returned fire but it was futile. Some were hit multiple times, their bodies spinning round like tops. Others tried to run, but their assailants had every angle covered. For Ruth, who was being sandwiched between Ernie and Kohl's dead body, the thirty second carefully planned assault felt like a lifetime. Then came the silence, the eerie aftermath of battle, the only sound was the occasional groan of a mortally wounded soldier seconds before death. Ruth broke the silence by pushing Kohl's dead body to one side. He rolled onto his back, eyes wide open staring into the canopy of the trees. Ernie, still in pain, with Ruth's assistance sat up, wondering what the hell had happened.

Slowly, one by one, from the cover of the trees and bushes, soldiers cautiously came out, weapons at the ready. Ernie recognised them straight away as Americans. One of them, presumably the commander, raised his hand; the others assumed the kneeling position. Some trained their weapons on Ernie and Ruth, others scanned the dead Germans for any signs of movement.

In a broad American accent, the commander instructed, 'Keep your hands where we can see them, no sudden moves.'

'I'm English,' Ernie called out.

Looking surprised but still with an air of caution the American replied, 'What the hell you doing this far forward?'

'I was wounded and captured, we were both on the run trying to get back to British lines.'

With a small smile, the American said, 'Well, it looks like we got here just in time.' The American officer raised two fingers first to his left eye then his right then spun his hand in a circle. His men knew exactly what he meant, some checked the dead Germans, the others took up all round defence. He then turned to a soldier with a Red Cross arm band, 'See what you can do for them Doc, looks like they have had a bit of an ordeal.'

The medic double timed over to them, while Ruth protectively held on to Ernie, 'If you're OK m'am I will have a look at your friend, he looks like he could do with some help.' 'Of course,' replied Ruth, and moved to one side out of the way. The officer gave Ruth a very haphazard salute then introduced himself, 'Good morning m'am, Captain James Nash, United States Army.'

'Pleased to make your acquaintance Captain,' Captain Nash instantly noticed Ruth's accent.

'Where you from m'am?'

'My parents are German Jews,' she told him. 'I fear they may have perished in the labour camps. The Nazis no longer recognise us as German citizens, and I no longer want to be associated with Germany.'

The officer nodded his head. 'Yes m'am, I can understand that, there are some terrible stories coming out of these concentration camps. Let's just hope they aren't all true'. Ruth's chin could be seen to physically drop. One of the things that had kept her going was that in her heart she still believed one day she would be reunited with her parents. The captain's eyes crossed to Ernie who was now on his knees. The medic had got his shirt undone and was wrapping a broad bandage tightly around his ribs.

'And you sir?' Ernie tried to stand, 'No, no, stay there till Doc's sorted you out.'

'Think he may have a couple of cracked ribs sir, hopefully nothing that won't heal,' said the medic.

Trying to get his breath, Ernie said, 'Corporal White, British 1st Airborne, I was captured at the Arnhem landings.'

'Jesus, that was months ago,' said the captain, 'Where the hell you been Corporal?'

'It's a long story sir, if it wasn't for Ruth,' he smiled at her, 'I wouldn't be here.'

'Well you can save it for when we get you back behind our front line, this place is swarming with Jerries. It's only a matter of days before they cave in completely, they will start breaking ranks and try to get as far away from Berlin as possible. We have orders to shoot on sight, especially those SS swine. Got themselves quite a reputation, no prisoners is what we heard.' The medic got up and helped Ernie to his feet, 'OK sir, he's good to go.' Ruth took hold of Ernie's arm to give him a little more stability. His dog tags were tight around the back of his neck, he was just about to pull them to the front when the captain said, 'You OK Corporal?'

Ernie diverted his hand to his ribs, 'Fine thank you sir,' replied Ernie. He had just remembered he still had Nickolaus Kesling's tags on and in his pocket, the Iron Cross Hitler had given him. After what he had just been told about the SS and taking no prisoners. It was probably a good idea to keep it to himself, for now at least.

'We left our Jeeps about four hundred yards back, think you can make it?'

'Yes sir, no problem,' said Ernie wincing a little. They set off, Ernie moved as quickly as his ribs allowed with Ruth under his arm for support. The Americans, vigilant as ever, maintained all-round defence as they made their way back to the vehicles.

Ernie slowly sat up straight and stretched out his lower back. Sitting still for so long had made his old joints seize up. 'That ride back in the Jeep wasn't much fun, I felt every pothole. Every bump was like another kick in the ribs. They were a good bunch of lads those yanks. They reminded me of my platoon, always having a laugh at each other's expense, but in a nice way if you know what I mean.'

Alex smiled, from his own military experience he knew exactly what the old man meant. Ernie again momentarily paused with his own thoughts, then he said, 'You see, when you're surrounded by death and destruction day in day out for weeks, sometimes months, if you don't laugh about it you'll go out of your mind. I could tell those lads had been through it, it was etched on their faces.'

Ernie looked up and half smiled. 'Anyway, enough of that. Once we got on the road it took us about an hour to get back to the Yank lines. The road was littered with the remains of the so called Third Reich, burnt out trucks and tanks. Bodies just left where they had fallen, it sticks in your mind, especially the civilians who were just trying to get away, the big shells and bombs in those days didn't pick their targets like they do today. My problem now was keeping hold of Ruth, at the end of the day I was still on active service. At some stage in the near future I would have to go back to my unit just like any other soldier. You see, although Ruth was a Jew she was still a German citizen, we decided the best thing to do was play the refugee card. Only problem was, there were so many other Germans, especially deserters, trying the same thing. Then I had an idea that hopefully would solve the problem once and for all.'

A few hundred yards down the road Ernie could see a make shift albeit heavily fortified barricade strewn across the road. The Jeep driver said, 'Home sweet home.' Then he looked over his shoulder at Ernie and Ruth and dazzled them with his perfect smile. 'Keep your eyes on the road soldier,' said Captain Nash, sitting next to him with one boot placed firmly on the dashboard.

'Finally a hot meal,' said the driver, the captain shook his head.

'For God's sake man, we've only been out for three days; anyone would think it had been a month.'

'It felt like two sir,' said the driver keeping his eyes fixed firmly on the barricade. They pulled up a few yards short, Captain Nash stood up in the Jeep so the men behind the barricade could clearly see him.

'You must remember me for Christ's sake, it's only been a few days,' A young soldier no more than about nineteen years old came running from behind the barrier and over to the Jeep, he quickly came to attention and saluted.

'Captain Nash sir, just had to be sure,' Nash shook his head and looked up in the air. The soldier looked at Ernie and Ruth, 'Can you vouch for these civilians sir?' That was it, Nash had had enough.

'THAT'S NO CIVILIAN, SOLDIER,' realising he was shouting he took a deep breath. 'That private is an escaped POW and his lady who have been to hell and back, NOW OPEN UP.'

'Yes sir, straight away.' The soldier quickly ran back; half a dozen men pushed the barricade to one side. Before it was even three quarters of its way across the road, one by one the Jeeps rolled in just missing both men and barricade debris.

When the last of the Jeeps was inside, the men again painstakingly pushed the barricade back into place and took up positions behind it. At the rear of the make shift compound a lorry laden with fuelled up jerry cans was the first port of call. The Jeeps made an orderly line, Captain Nash stood up in the lead Jeep and looked back at his men, 'Get them fuelled up boys and give them the once over, I got a feeling we aren't going to be here that long.' He jumped out of the Jeep and looked at Ernie and Ruth, 'I bet you two could do with a good meal and something warm to drink,'

'Sounds good to me sir,' said Ernie.

'Give me two minutes and I'll get someone to look after you. I have to report to the colonel. He'll probably send for you to be debriefed. You've probably acquired more information than you actually realise. Once that's sorted we'll try and contact your outfit, they'll be pleased to see you.'

Ernie smiled, 'Pleased to see me? They think I'm dead.'

'After what you've told me I'm surprised you aren't.' They all laughed, 'Two minutes,' said Captain Nash then he turned and walked off in the direction of a cluster of large tents.

Ernie turned to Ruth, who looked cold, 'Come here,' he said as he put his arms around her, squeezing her tight. 'The worst is over now darling,'

'I hope so,' replied Ruth nuzzling into his chest.

True to his word, within a few minutes Captain Nash appeared out of nowhere, 'Kowaski,' he shouted at a group of soldiers trying to keep out the way behind a pile of empty jerry cans.

'Yes sir,' came the reply from one of the men, wiping his hands on an oily rag. The young soldier came running over; his crew cut was so tight he was virtually bald, which meant not only was his face dirty but also the top of his head. He came to attention in front of the captain.

'At ease soldier,' Kowaski relaxed. 'I want you to take our guests to the cook house, make sure they are fed and watered, look after them and make them welcome.'

'Yes sir,' replied the young soldier. 'This way folks,' Ernie and Ruth followed him across the compound towards the cookhouse.

As they got half way across the captain called after them, 'And Kowaski…'

Again the soldier stopped and looked back, 'Yes sir?' The captain shook his head, 'Get cleaned up.'

The young man smiled and got on with his task. A good hour later Ernie and Ruth, still in the cookhouse, sat back on their chairs, Ernie had undone the button on his trouser waist band. They had both eaten far too much and were paying for it. Kowaski had left them to it, telling them to stay put and he would come back for them once he had completed the rest of his duties. All they needed now was somewhere to lay their heads for a few hours and their contentment would be complete. Unfortunately it wasn't to be. Kowaski suddenly appeared at the cookhouse entrance. 'Hey you guys had enough to eat?' Kowaski smiled, by their appearance he was stating the obvious. 'Captain Nash asked me to take you over to the colonel's tent as soon as you're ready.' Ernie and Ruth both looked at each other as if to say 'Now?'

'Come on girl,' said Ernie, 'One more push.' They both got up straightened their clothing and followed Kowaski out the tent and across the compound. Inside the tent a group of six officers stood in a circle drinking coffee, discussing what they referred to as the final push. Kowaski entered the tent first and quickly came to attention.

The conversation quickly came to an end; they all turned to look at Captain Nash's guests. A little sheepishly, Ernie and Ruth stood by the tent entrance, Nash broke the silence. 'Thanks Kowaski, that will be all,' Kowaski saluted and turned on the spot. As he looked at Ernie he raised his eyebrows in a kind of a silent good luck; then he walked out.

'Please come in,' said Nash. He turned to the colonel, 'These are the couple I told you about, got in a whole load of trouble with a German patrol, lucky we came along when we did.' Colonel John McKinley stepped forward. He looked considerably older than he actually was. At just forty four years his white hair and moustache didn't do his physical prowess any justice. He had led from the front since the American intervention in the war. He spoke to Ernie first, 'Your name sir?' Ernie immediately came to attention.

'Private Ernie White, 1st British Airborne.'

'At ease soldier,' Ernie relaxed a little.'

'And you m'am?'

'Ruth Zimmerman, I am a nurse sir.'

'Well, from what Captain Nash tells me you have both had quite an ordeal.' He turned to his fellow officers and introduced them, 'This is Captain Turner,' the officer nodded, 'Lieutenants Phelps and Kramer,' they both also nodded, 'Captain Nash you already know, and our Brigade Chaplain Captain Forester,' the chaplain gently smiled. 'You can appreciate there is a lot going on at the moment. Before I ship you back to your own people, Private White and Miss Zimmerman I'd like you to give as much information as you can to...' he scanned his officers. 'To Lieutenant Phelps, anything you can remember, troop numbers, movement, even the morale of the people you came into contact with. Artillery tanks, especially anything that's dug in, you know what I mean Private.'

'Any way we can help sir, we will,' said Ernie enthusiastically.

'Good man,' replied the colonel, 'the sooner we all go home the better.' The chaplain suddenly spoke up, 'I'd like to get involved Colonel with that debrief if you don't mind.'

'That's fine with me George.' He turned to Phelps, 'Sooner rather than later Lieutenant.'

'I'll get straight on it sir,' replied Phelps. The rest of the officers went back to their discussions. Ernie, Ruth, Lieutenant Phelps and the chaplain went to find a quiet tent within the compound where they could talk. They finally decided the quietest place where they wouldn't be interrupted was the chaplain's quarters. Phelps and the chaplain sat on one side of a small table, Ernie and Ruth on the other. Phelps placed a note pad on the table and sat back, 'Right then, let's start from the beginning.' Ernie started right from when his small band of brothers were sent on the reconnaissance mission. He held back nothing. At times the chaplain intervened, seeing that the psychological wounds where far from healed, but he got through it.

'That is an amazing story Ernie,' said Phelps dropping his military front. He looked at Ruth, 'Is there anything you can add Miss Zimmerman,'

'Please call me Ruth.'

'Certainly Ruth,' said Phelps with a smile.

'I just want to know if I will be sent back. There's nothing for me there. My parents were sent to the work camps, if my father hadn't anticipated what was going to happen I would probably have ended up in the same place,' she lowered her head.

The chaplain spoke up, 'We aren't going to lie to you Ruth, the stories that we are hearing from these concentration camps aren't good.'

Ernie spoke up, 'I want her to come back to England with me.'

'There are rules on refugees, displaced people as they like to refer to them, we can't really answer that one.'

'There's got to be a way,' said Ernie, 'Got to be.' Phelps stood up followed by the chaplain, 'Right what we'll do is contact the British and find out where they would like us to send you; in the meantime relax, you have certainly earned it by that story.' They left Ernie and Ruth with their thoughts. Neither said a word for quite some time.

Suddenly Ernie jumped to his feet. Ruth looked startled.

'What's wrong?' said Ruth.

'Nothing,' replied Ernie. 'I've got it.'

'Got what?' said Ruth.

'Marry me.' Ruth looked flabbergasted. Ernie got down on one knee.

'I was going to wait till we were back in England, but it looks like it can't wait.'

'How?' asked Ruth,

'That officer's a chaplain isn't he? He can do it.'

'But...'

'Never mind but, just say yes.'

Ruth put her hands on her forehead; she didn't expect to be proposed to like this. 'I know it's not perfect,' said Ernie, 'But Ruth Zimmerman I love you, I can't imagine life without you. If that's not a good enough reason to get married I don't know what is.'

Ruth felt tears welling up in her eyes, 'Yes, yes of course I'll marry you.' Ernie jumped to his feet, 'Stay there.' Ernie ran out of the tent. All he had to do now was persuade the chaplain to perform the ceremony before he was sent back to re-join what was left of his unit.

'You old devil,' said Alex with a broad smile on his face. Ernie tried to resist but couldn't help a cheeky grin in return.

'I don't mind saying myself, at the time I thought it was a great idea, but it wasn't that easy. We finally managed to persuade the chaplain, and then he had to persuade the colonel. Unfortunately we still had to go our own ways, you see the British didn't have much time for Jewish refugees after the war, but once we were married they had to listen.' Ernie paused for a moment forming a mental picture, 'If you could have seen her that day, she looked absolutely beautiful. I don't know how those Yanks do it, but they have a knack of getting stuff out of nowhere. When those lads heard the chaplain was going to marry us, we couldn't believe what they did.'

Ernie and Ruth were sat outside the chaplain's tent. It wasn't just his accommodation, it was a makeshift chapel for anyone that needed to talk or pray as the case may be. Kowaski, the soldier that had been assigned to them earlier came over.

'Hey you guys the colonel wants to see you.' They both got up. 'Is it true?' said Kowaski.

'Is what true?' replied Ernie, confused.

'The chaplain's going to wed you guys,' Ernie and Ruth both looked at each other and smiled, turning to Kowaski Ernie said, 'Can't keep no secrets in this camp.'

'Congratulations!' said Kowaski in a loud exuberant voice as he grabbed Ernie's hand and vigorously shook it. Then he did the same to Ruth, 'You'll have to excuse me m'am, but it's not every day something like this happens in a war zone and it kind of makes us remember what life was like back home, well at least for a little while.' Ernie felt that he knew exactly what the soldier meant, 'What's your name?' asked Ernie.

'Kowaski,' Ernie smiled 'I know that, your first name.' 'Oh, it's Zack, but I can't remember the last time anybody called me by it.'

'Well you will now. Listen Zack, we are going to need a couple of witnesses to make it all legal and that.'

'What, you want me to?'

'If you don't mind,' the soldier's face looked like he had just been told he was going home. 'Yes sir, I would be honoured for sure,' his accent was even more pronounced with his excitement. Still hyper he turned, 'Listen guys, I have a few things to sort out,' as he scurried away he turned and called back, 'Don't forget, the colonel wants to see you in his tent straight away.'

As he disappeared across the compound Ruth said, 'What a strange man.'

'He's harmless,' said Ernie, 'Come on, we'd better not keep the colonel waiting.'

Arm in arm they made their way to the colonel's tent. They stood in the doorway. The colonel was sat alone at his makeshift desk, just in front him were opened maps of the surrounding area. With his elbows on the desk his thumb and index finger slowly massaged a furrowed brow. With no way of knocking Ernie just coughed a little louder than normal. The colonel raised his eyes from his maps, 'Ah, come in you two.' Ernie, automatically falling into military mode, came to attention in front of the desk. 'Please stand easy Private White.'

'The chaplain and I discussed your request, and I don't mind telling you at first I wasn't very keen. This is a war zone, and if it all goes to plan my men will be pushing all the way to Berlin in less than twenty four hours, and the chances are they aren't all going home.' The colonel paused letting the thought sink in. 'With that in mind letting them see some sort of normality, if that's what you can call it; might just take away a bit of the tension. So this is what's going to happen. At twenty hundred hours the chaplain will perform your little ceremony in his tent. The men will obviously be aware of what's going on but it will be low key, you got that?'

'Yes sir,' said Ernie. Ruth raised her arm like a frightened child asking a question in a class room.

'May we use two of the men as witnesses, for the legal side of things, you know?' The colonel looked at her then raised his eyebrows. 'Yes, I think we can stretch to that,' Ruth smiled and shuffled around on the spot as she held on to Ernie's arm. The colonel's blank expression did not change, but if the truth be known he was pleased to see something good amongst such hardship and sorrow. 'Right that's all sorted then, I have arranged transport in the morning to take you both to a safer zone. The probability is at some time in the very near future you will be separated. I'm afraid the outcome of that is out of my hands.'

Ernie understandingly nodded his head.

'Well then,' said the colonel, getting up from his chair, 'If I can be the first to congratulate you both.' He extended his hand first to Ernie then to Ruth, 'I wish you both every happiness for the future, hopefully in a more peaceful environment.'

'I'll second that sir,' replied Ernie, the colonel almost cracked a smile; but then simply nodded his head, took a deep breath and sat back down. They both sensed this was their cue to leave, and like backing off from royalty, they took a couple of steps backwards, turned and walked out of the tent. The colonel by this time was once more absorbed in his maps.

Later that afternoon, as they had no accommodation for the night, Captain Nash offered them his tent; he told them he could mess in with the lieutenants, it wouldn't be a problem. Pleased with the way everything was panning out, Ruth asked Captain Nash if he would be their second witness at the ceremony. A little apprehensively he agreed. After his conversation with the colonel the last thing he wanted was to get on the wrong side of his superior officer. A small delegation of men fronted by Kowaski came over to the tent holding a large box. Ruth nudged Ernie. 'There are some soldiers outside; I think they want us.' Ernie pulled back the door flap, 'Everything alright lads?'

Kowaski held out the box. 'We put a few things together for the lady. The guys got it from some deserted houses nearby, thought she might like them.'

'Thank you,' said Ernie, a little puzzled as to what might be in there. Again he acknowledged them with a nod of his head then went back in the tent.

'It's for you.'

'Me?' said Ruth sounding very surprised, 'What on earth could they have for me?'

Ernie placed the box down on a makeshift table. The lid was tight. Ruth prized her fingers under the edge to free it. After a little struggle it popped open. Peering inside she said, 'What the?' with both hands she took hold of some red silky material and pulled it out of the box. Holding it up in front of her, it was a dress and very close, if not exactly her size. Her face was a picture, 'How did they get hold of this?'

Ernie laughed, 'They're American's, they can get anything.' She draped the dress over her arm and again looked in the box. There was a set of hair brushes, a hand held mirror, some lipstick, a pair of shoes, some dress jewellery, a small bottle of perfume and a bar of scented soap that could be smelled as soon as the lid had been removed. She meticulously examined the items one by one; it had been a long time since she had any creature comforts or clean clothes let alone a beautiful dress. The tears welled in her eyes; Ernie could see how emotional she was. 'Come here,' he said putting his arms around her and squeezing her tightly 'Just think, another few hours and you'll be Mrs Ruth White.'

Suddenly she pulled away, 'And you aren't supposed to see my dress.'

Ernie put his hands over his eyes, 'Never seen a thing,' they both laughed; it had been a long time since they had shared real heartfelt laughter.

Ruth spent the rest of the afternoon pampering herself. Kowaski somehow acquired a large tin bath and after numerous journeys to and fro with a large water jug, he had partially filled it with warm water. After being on the run for so long, the warmth and relaxation combined with the scented soap made the word bliss an understatement. Ernie received clean fatigues and boots. Being very secretive about the way he had received his Iron Cross, he wrapped it in a piece of clean cloth and transferred it carefully to the pocket of his new trousers. Half an hour before the scheduled time of their little ceremony, Ernie went over to the tent that had been Ruth's domain for the afternoon. He didn't want to just walk in, in case she was still dressing. Standing by the closed flap of the tent Ernie shouted, 'It's only me, can I come in?' No answer. Again he called, 'Ruth, can I come in?' When there was no answer for the second time he quickly opened the flap. As he looked in what he saw stopped him in his tracks. Ruth was stood facing him some three or four yards away, her hair was combed down. In the time he had known her it had always been in plaits, she was more beautiful than ever. Her long blonde hair glistened on her shoulders; the dress looked as if it had been made for her. For a few moments he was stuck for words, he just stood there with his mouth half open.

'It's not that bad is it?' asked Ruth dismayed by his silence.

Ernie shook his head, 'Bad?' he smiled. 'You look absolutely beautiful.' She started to blush.

'I don't know about that,' she said her face already reddening.

Ernie walked over and took hold of both her hands. 'I'm the luckiest bloke in the world.' Not wanting to mess up her hair or clothing he raised her hands up to his mouth and gently kissed them. Ruth took a deep breath as the emotion of the moment almost brought her to tears. He gently squeezed her hands and said, 'Come on, I think they're waiting for us.' Everything went perfectly; Captain Nash and Kowaski played out their parts as if it had been rehearsed many times. Kowaski even managed to come up with a couple of make do wedding rings for the chaplain to bless. Where he got them from, they never found out. They left the chaplain's tent to rapturous applause from a large group of soldiers that, against orders had gathered outside. As Captain Nash had kindly given up his accommodation for the evening, Kowaski with a little help from his friends, had prepared a large makeshift bed. At the side on a small rickety old table stood two glasses and a bottle of wine. It didn't look much but meant everything to Ernie and Ruth, as it was probably their first and last night together as man and wife for some time to come. Ernie thanked everyone, especially Kowaski for their thoughtful kindness, then they retired to the relative privacy of their tent.

'Sounds like they did you proud,' said Alex.

'Proud, that's an understatement' said Ernie, 'Couldn't fault them. For those few hours together we actually started to forget there was a war on. Of course, we still knew we were going to be separated and for how long we didn't know,' Ernie paused in thought. 'Kind of took the edge off it a bit, but it was wonderful while it lasted. Years after the war we tried to locate Kowaski and Captain Nash, you know, our witnesses.'

Alex gave a knowing nod. 'It would have been nice to see them in peace time or even just send a letter to thank them for everything they had done for us. Turns out that last push to Berlin they were both killed, ambushed by a bunch of kids on the outskirts of the city. The majority of the German army had accepted the inevitable by now, but pockets of hard-line Nazis fought to the last man. These Hitler Youth kids, as young as fourteen, had made a pledge to defend the city to their last breath and a lot of them did just that, terrible waste. Anyway it turned out the colonel wasn't such a grouse as we first thought, he did us proud too. We didn't know at the time but he had pulled a few strings and got Ruth assigned to a Red Cross hospital unit that was looking after back loaded British servicemen. It gave us hope if nothing else, I wrote down as much information as I could that might help her find me, but I knew it was going to be hard when the time came.

The sound of voices and vehicle engines woke Ernie. Ruth was sleeping soundly, entwined in his arms. It was still dark, the amount of activity outside the tent meant something important was happening. Trying his best not to wake her, he slowly took his arms from around her and edged himself out the bed. There was a chill in the air. Quickly he pulled on his trousers and vest, then pulled the flap of the tent across, peering out into the darkness. It seemed as if every vehicle in the compound was moving at the same time, all with an urgent destination. From what he could see the camp was being packed away in its entirety. He closed the flap to try and reduce the sound but it was futile. Ruth began to stir. With eyes half open she stretched her arms above her head. As her eyes came into focus she saw Ernie and smiled. 'Morning Mrs White,' said Ernie endearingly. She pulled the blanket back and beckoned him with her arms to come back to bed. Seeing her naked form and feeling the chill in the room he didn't need telling twice. He quickly slipped out of his clothes, climbed back into bed and, not knowing the next time they would be in each other's arms, they made love. As they lay in bed and each with their own thoughts, a voice called out, 'Sorry to disturb you guys, but all the tents are being dismantled, like very soon.'

Ernie and Ruth looked at each other, Ernie called out, 'Righto we're getting dressed, give us a few minutes.'

'OK guys, the colonel wants to see you before we pull out,' replied the voice. Ten minutes later they were dressed. They quickly swilled their hands and face in a bowl with a jug of water that had been put in the tent for them the previous evening. Ruth gathered up the gifts the soldiers had given her, combed her hair through and quickly plaited it with an expertise Ernie could only marvel at.

'What?' asked Ruth wondering why Ernie was staring at her.

'Nothing,' said Ernie trying to contain the sheer happiness he felt at that moment in time. 'We had better go and see what the colonel wants. We don't want to rub him up the wrong way after all he has done for us.' Ernie agreed, they gathered up the remainder of their things. As they left the tent, lined up outside were row after row of Jeeps fully laden with personal kit, ammunition and fuel in jerry cans just in case it didn't go completely to plan.

As they crossed the compound some soldiers greeted them with a nod, some distant ones wolf whistled. Others continued with their tasks oblivious to their presence, their minds preoccupied with what the rest of the day would bring. Ernie held on to Ruth's arm as the occasional Jeep got a little too close for comfort trying to manoeuvre into position within the convoy of vehicles.

No sooner had they left Captain Nash's tent, it was already being dismantled. However, directly in front of them colonel McKinley's tent stood untouched; the division's central hub of orders and communications. The flap of the tent was pulled back and secured; the colonel was stood behind his map table, his thumb and index finger shaping the line of his moustache, aiding his thought process.

Ernie and Ruth once again stood in the doorway.

'Excuse me sir,' said Ernie, 'You wanted to see us?'

Snapping out of his trance the colonel looked up, 'Both of you please come in.' They made their way over to the table and Ernie looked down at the map. It was covered in directional arrows. At the end of each arrow on the western approach to Berlin was a British or American flag, on the east side of the city was a long line of Russian flags. There were still a few swastikas on the edges of the city, presumably the last points of strong German resistance. The colonel walked away from the map and picked up a packet of cigarettes,

'Smoke?'

'No thank you sir,' said Ernie.

'M'am?' Ruth just shook her head slightly. The colonel tapped the packet and a single cigarette popped up. He put it in his mouth and from out of thin air he struck a match, almost like a party piece. He took a long draw and then slowly blew out the smoke, his only means of stress relief. 'I hope everything went well for you both yesterday.'

'Excellent sir,' said Ernie, 'Very much appreciated.'

'That's good,' replied the colonel, 'I have a Jeep waiting to take you back to the British lines, you m'am are going to a Red Cross field hospital. It was the best I could do at short notice, the men there are being shipped back to Britain. Under the circumstances I think once you are separated it's your best chance of getting there.' Ruth smiled, she wanted to give him a hug but it didn't feel like the right thing to do at that moment. Instead she said, 'Thank you colonel, for everything,'

'It's my pleasure m'am, least I could do after what my officers tell me you have both been through these last few months.'

'It's been challenging to say the least,' said Ernie, the colonel nodded and again drew hard on his cigarette. As the smoke escaped his lungs he said, 'Well then have a safe journey and good luck.' Ernie came to attention and saluted, the colonel returned a less enthusiastic salute.

Ruth couldn't contain her gratitude any longer, she stepped forward kissed his cheek and thanked him.

The colonel visibly blushed, 'Right then best be on your way,' he said trying to quell his embarrassment. As they turned and left the tent the colonel privately smiled to himself and went back to his map.

Already waiting outside the tent a lone soldier sat in his Jeep, tapping out some musical rhythm on the edge of the steering wheel. Spotting them, he raised his hand, 'Over here folks,' he called out. They walked over to the Jeep, 'Are you taking us back to the British lines?' 'Yes sir, and the lady has to be taken to the Red Cross hospital about eight miles back. We have to go now, these guys are moving out in an hour and I don't fancy making that approach to Berlin on my own.'

'Understood,' said Ernie. Ruth climbed into the back of the Jeep. Ernie sat in the front with the driver's machine gun lying across his lap.

'Stay sharp,' said the driver, 'There are still some small pockets of resistance on the roads.' He looked over his shoulder at Ruth, 'Hold tight m'am, these Jeeps aren't the most comfortable of vehicles at the best of times, let alone for a lady.' With that he sped off across the compound, his intention to get the task done as fast as possible.

The journey went without a hitch. All the same Ernie constantly scanned the surrounding woods and burnt out houses, just in case a lone sniper or fleeing deserter saw them as any easy target for transport out of there. Ernie had told Ruth to keep low in the back, a request he didn't need to repeat. The driver kept up his speed, except for when they passed burnt out vehicles strewn across the road; caution seemed the best option at these times. Within half an hour they arrived at the makeshift hospital. There was no sign of any security, the perimeter was completely unguarded. British casualties there far outnumbered any other nationalities, but there were Americans and a few Germans. The large red cross symbol on top of their makeshift ambulances and tents hopefully kept them safe from any accidental air attacks. As they pulled up, the driver turned to Ernie, 'We have to be quick with our goodbyes, it's taken longer than I expected.' Ernie gave him an understanding nod and climbed out the Jeep.

A man in an apron some yards away stood by a large tent, washing his hands in a bucket of water. Seeing them pull up he grabbed a towel and starting walking towards them. Ernie took hold of Ruth's hand and helped her out of the Jeep. From his trouser pocket Ernie pulled out a neatly folded piece of paper, 'Here,' he gave it to Ruth. 'Everything about me is written on this piece of paper, home address, army number, anything and everything is written down on there.' She took it and held it tightly in her hand, her eyes filling with tears.

'Don't cry,' said Ernie with emotion in his voice, 'we will be back together soon.'

She nodded and swallowed hard, 'I love you Ernie White.' He held her tightly.

'Morning,' said the man in the apron, his authoritative voice made Ernie correctly assume he was an officer. 'Captain Simmonds, British Army Medical Corps.' Ernie quickly came to attention and saluted.

'Morning sir, Private White, Airborne, this is my wife Ruth, she has a civilian attachment to you, Colonel McKinley arranged it.' The captain turned to Ruth, 'Yes, I wondered when you were going to get here. The colonel's message only had praise for you, we are really short of good nurses,' Ruth smiled through the tears in her eyes. 'Time's up,' said the driver, 'Please take good care of her sir,' said Ernie looking straight at the captain, who offered him his hand, 'That, Private White, is guaranteed.' Ernie shook his hand. Impatiently the driver said, 'I'm going Mack, with or without you.' Ernie took the hint and jumped into the front of the Jeep. The driver spun the Jeep round, turning his head Ernie looked into Ruth's eyes. Without saying it, he mouthed 'I love you', through her tears again she smiled. As they drove off Ernie looked behind, keeping eye contact as long as he could. Once out of sight he sat with his eyes fixed on the road ahead, no longer concerned with pending attacks, just lost in his thoughts of Ruth.

Alex shook his head, 'Must have been really hard Ernie, just driving away like that.'

'That's an understatement,' said Ernie, 'It was like having me right arm cut off. I've got to be honest it's the only time I ever felt like,' Ernie paused. 'Deserting?' asked Alex, 'You said it,' Ernie was embarrassed at even the thought of it. 'Once I got back to my outfit I felt a little better, the medics said my war was over. The injuries I got that day in the barn never really healed, well properly anyway. I had to have another couple of operations on my leg a few years later. Something about my knee not lining up, it was starting to throw me back out see. Anyway all I could think about at the time was Ruth and getting back to England.'

The Jeep pulled up in front of a makeshift barrier surrounded by sand bags stacked above waist height. A military policeman with sergeant stripes on his arm cautiously stepped forward. On top of the sand bags four rifle muzzles pointed straight at them. Any sudden move would have been their last. 'Can I see your papers please?' asked the MP. The driver slowly put his hand inside his jacket and pulled out some documentation. Ernie stayed well clear of the machine gun perched on the dashboard. The MP slowly read the paperwork and then looked over the top of the document at Ernie.

'Pleased to have you back Private White.'

'Pleased to be here,' said Ernie.

'Open up,' said the MP.

'That's OK Mack, I'll drop him here, I'm in kind of a rush.' Ernie climbed out the Jeep, and, offering his hand to the driver he said, 'Thanks for the ride.'

The driver shook his hand, 'You're welcome.' With that he spun the Jeep round and sped off in the direction he came from. The soldiers behind the sandbags lowered their weapons and stood down.

'Right then,' said the MP, 'I'll take you over to HQ, I'm sure they have one or two questions for you; follow me.' They both edged round the barrier, 'Corporal Watts, you're in charge.'

'Yes Sergeant,' replied the soldier as he took a packet of cigarettes out of his top pocket and leaned against the sandbags. The sergeant set off, his marching speed a little too fast for Ernie. It wasn't till that moment that Ernie realised the injuries he had sustained to his leg could be a real problem. His ankle was still sore but that had been just a sprain from when they had made their get away from the German patrol. The pain in his thigh was something else.

The adjacent field was lined with marquee-like tents and at the far end there were half a dozen prefabricated buildings. The sergeant marched over to the buildings; Ernie doubled his speed to catch him up.

'Wait here, I'll see if the major wants to see you before you get settled in.' Ernie was just pleased to stop for a moment, his thigh was throbbing like mad. Within a couple of minutes the sergeant came back out, 'Major Carter said he will arrange your debrief for 11:00 hours.' The sergeant looked at his watch, 'It's 09:30, you have time to get billeted. Follow me.' Again the sergeant set off at a pace Ernie couldn't maintain, 'We had some other Airborne lads in just the other day, similar story, separated from their outfit. I'll put you in with them; no doubt you'll all have something in common.' They walked along the line of tents and at the one before the end he stopped. 'Last partition on the right, any free bed is yours, cook house is behind the tents; if you're quick they might have a bit of breakfast left. Happy?'

'Yes, thank you sergeant,' the sergeant nodded, turned, and walked off in the direction of the main gate. As he did so, in a loud commanding voice, he called back, 'Don't be late, debrief HQ 11:00 hours.'

Ernie smiled and shook his head. Under his breath he said, 'Sergeants, all the same.'

The tent was deceptively spacious. It was partitioned into six sections. He followed the partitions till the last opening on the right and turned in. There were eight beds, three were occupied with sleeping or just relaxing men. On the fourth a soldier sat cleaning his boots. As Ernie took a step inside the soldier looked up. His mouth dropped open, 'Oh my God, well if it isn't Chalky White.' The other three men jumped up on their beds, equally as shocked to hear Ernie's name. Ernie smiled, 'Carl Sullivan, you old devil.' 'We thought you were dead,' said Sullivan. Ernie laughed, 'So did I once or twice.' The other men got up; one by one they embraced him, brothers in arms, all with their own stories to tell.

For a good hour they discussed their fortunes and misfortunes. A very sombre mood fell on them when Ernie recounted the incident in the barn. So many good men lost in a matter of minutes. Before they all became too morose, Sullivan jumped up from his bed.

'I bet you're starving Chalky.'

'I could eat for sure,' he replied. One of the other men, a broad shouldered, heavily muscled Yorkshireman called Frank Pickering looked Ernie up and down. 'You look like you've lost some weight Chalky. You sure you haven't been in one of those work camps with those poor bloody Jewish people?' They all laughed, 'Ha-ha,' said Ernie sarcastically, 'Fit as a butcher's dog me, now you going to show me where this cook house is or what?'

Without warning, at lightning speed Pickering leapt forward grabbing Ernie by the shoulders. Typically the kind of horseplay expected from front line combat soldiers. He squeezed Ernie with one of his huge arms. Ernie tried to shake him off, but it was futile. With his other hand Pickering annoyingly messed up Ernie's hair and walked him out of the tent. As he released him he laughed out loud and said, 'Come on Chalky let's get some food inside ya.' Still clowning about, they all went over to the cookhouse. With Ernie just arriving in camp, the duty chef took one of his staff members off the dinnertime preparation to make him something. As Ernie tucked into a meal of sausage meat, scrambled egg and a hunk of bread, the rest of the lads told him about their exploits on the way to Arnhem. How they barely escaped with their lives and, more to the point, how many were killed or captured. Ernie suddenly stopped eating, 'Shit, what time is it?'

Sullivan looked at his watch. 'Just after eleven, why you got a date or something?' Ernie stood up, 'Holy shit, I was supposed to be at a debrief with some major at eleven.' He jumped from behind the bench, 'See you later lads, got to run.' With that he doubled out of the tent and across the field in the direction of the HQ buildings. Sullivan and Pickering both looked at Ernie's plate then at each other, 'Waste not want not,' said Sullivan. Within seconds Ernie's plate looked like it had just been washed.

As Ernie approached the HQ buildings he slowed down to get his breath, annoyed with himself for letting time get the better of him. He was never late; his policy had always been fifteen minutes early rather than one minute late. He took one more deep breath, knocked the door and walked in. There were two desks to his right, both stacked up with documentation of one form or another. To his left there was a line of chairs, just like a reception waiting room. The first of the two desks was occupied by a clerk, painfully thin, with small round rimmed glasses and just a few wisps of hair left on his head. He looked up over the top of his glasses, 'Can I help you?'

'Private White, I was told to report here at 11:00 hours to be debriefed.'

Clearly annoyed, the clerk raised his left arm and looked at his watch, 'It's nine minutes past.'

Ernie had taken an instant dislike to the man, he said nothing, he just stared back at him refusing to be intimidated by this jumped up little jobsworth. After a painful few seconds of silence the clerk said, 'Take a seat, the major is busy at the moment. Captain Williams is due back in camp before lunch time, he will probably deal with you.' The clerk went back to his paperwork. Ernie took a step backwards towards the chairs. Is he trying to wind me up? he wondered. After what he had been through, if this pen pusher thought he was going to give him a hard time, he had another thing coming. The clerk didn't look up, but he must have felt Ernie's eyes boring into his head.

Patiently Ernie waited. He had nothing else to do and it was warm and dry. After about fifteen minutes the office door to his left opened just a fraction. It sounded as if someone was whispering behind the door. As the door was pulled open, a very tall man looking flushed and dishevelled stood to one side of the door frame.

'Thank you Miss Marsh, if you could get that typed up for me ASAP.' A very attractive black haired young woman stepped out of the office holding a pad and pen. Ernie struggled to keep a straight face; he thought to himself, I wouldn't mind reading that memo once it's written up. She edged round the empty desk obviously embarrassed, trying not to make eye contact. She sat down and started re-arranging the files. The clerk raised his head from his work.

'Private White, sir, arrived in camp this morning. He needs to be debriefed sir, before the medical officer can declare him fit or unfit for service as the case may be.'

The officer looked at Ernie who was still eyeballing the clerk; Ernie quickly stood up and came to attention, 'Stand at ease Private White.' He walked over to Ernie and offered him his hand, 'Pleased to meet you. Major Carter, I read the brief from General McKinley. It seems you have quite a story to tell.' Ernie's expression said it all. The major smiled. 'You'll find it a little more relaxed here than what you are used to, with the exception of our own Sergeant Thomas. You may have met him on the gate.' Ernie smiled, 'Yes sir.' 'He's a good man.' said Carter, 'old school, you just have to accept the way he is, he means well.' Ernie gave an understanding nod. 'Come into the office.' He stepped to one side and

Ernie walked in. Carter turned to the clerk, 'As soon as Captain Williams arrives send him in will you?'

'Yes sir,' said the clerk without looking up. Carter glanced at the young woman, she half looked up, he winked and smiled. Like an embarrassed schoolgirl she blushed, half smiled, and went back to her work. Carter closed the door.

'Take a seat Private White.'

Ernie thanked him, pulled a chair over and sat down.

'Did I see a limp there, White?'

'Yes sir, when we first landed outside Arnhem I was sent on a reconnaissance mission. We walked into a German patrol, all hell let loose. I was the only one that survived to my knowledge. That was the start of quite an ordeal.'

A knock on the door interrupted, 'Excuse me White. Come in.' It was Captain Williams.

'Aah, Captain Williams come on in.' Williams closed the door behind him, 'This is Private White, he was captured by a German patrol months back.'

'Sorry sir, that's not quite true, you see they thought I was a German soldier by the name of Nickolaus Kesling.'

'Sounds intriguing,' said Williams pulling up a seat.

'Well it's a long story,' said Ernie.

'Fire away,' said Carter, 'we've got all afternoon.'

Ernie's audience at the supermarket had slowly dwindled, so that only Alex remained, enthralled by the story. The majority had succumbed to their stomachs calling out for Sunday lunch. 'That was that really,' said Ernie sitting up to straighten out his back.

Alex shook his head. 'I bet they couldn't believe what they were hearing.'

'Well, as I remember, the captain kept scratching his head, but I'm not sure if that was my story, or he had just been in the field too long, although they did start paying closer attention when I showed them my Iron Cross.'

Alex laughed, 'So how did you get back here and more to the point how did you find Ruth?' 'Hmm, now that's another story.' As the memories came flooding back to the forefront of his mind the old veteran smiled.

Alex looked at his watch. 'Come on then, I've got another half an hour, you can't leave it at that.'

'You're a glutton for punishment,' said Ernie, pleased really that someone could take such an interest in an old man's stories.

'Well after the debrief they sent me to see the medical officer. He picked up on my limp straight away. I had to strip down for a full medical. When he saw my leg he complimented the German doctors for their handiwork. As far as active service was concerned, my days were over. He told me the best I would get after the war was a desk job.' Ernie paused, looked down and shook his head. 'Couldn't see myself doing something like that, I mean I'd been active all my life. Before the army it was football and a bit of boxing, anyway I don't mind saying it depressed me somewhat, but sometimes you just have to accept the inevitable. If I had to do a desk job, so be it. A few days later we heard the Russians had taken Berlin and Hitler was already dead. Turned out he committed suicide in his bunker some days before the Russians took control. The so-called Third Reich had fallen apart; we heard they were surrendering all over the place. All I could think about was Ruth and how I was going to find her. The camp I was in got wrapped up late April 1945, I got shipped home on a medical convoy. Every time I saw a nurse with blonde hair I'd dash over thinking I'd found her, but each time I was disappointed. I just hoped and prayed somehow she had made it back to England.'

April turned to May and, still classified as unfit for active service Ernie was given leave to go home to see his parents. He hoped his brothers were also on leave. Only weeks earlier they were still under the impression he was missing in action and feared the worst, but his mother never gave up hope. Call it what you will, a woman's intuition; when the letter arrived saying that he was safe and well and back in England his father jumped for joy but she hardly batted an eye lid, 'Told you so.' She never was one for showing her emotions, but privately shed a tear of happiness and relief.

Ernie planned to spend a couple of days at home and then use the opportunity to start his search for Ruth. His parents were stunned when he told them he was married, but at the same time were over the moon to hear his story of how they met and what they had been through together. His mother told him it was a real testament of their love for one another and again, instinctively, she knew he would find her. Public communication was still poor but it was improving. Ernie made enquiries through military and civilian channels, but drew a blank. So many people had been displaced, it was like looking for a needle in a haystack.

Just by chance, an old friend Ernie hadn't seen since the start of the war bumped into him in the corner shop. He was also on medical leave; he told Ernie he had picked up some shrapnel from a mine, literally days before it was all over and had been sent back home straight away, believing he would never walk again. They had removed as much of the shrapnel as they could, but it was going to be a long time before he was up and about. Well, he proved them wrong. Within three weeks he was walking around. They had sent him to convalesce in Hampshire, just outside the town of Borden. Sharing a little boyish bravado, he told Ernie about all the beautiful nurses he had seen in these makeshift hospitals and convalescence homes.

Ernie thanked him for the information and wished him a speedy recovery. It was a long shot but he had to start somewhere, he felt that if he had to rely on the authorities to locate Ruth, he would wait forever. After explaining the situation to his parents, they both supported him one hundred percent and told him life was too short, they gave him their support. The next day he would catch a train down south and start looking for his needle in a haystack.

Bright and early Ernie set off with nothing more than an overnight bag and a packed lunch his mother had prepared for him. He didn't have any train times, he just thought he would take his chance. He didn't really have a specific plan, just head towards the town of Bordon and see what developed. With the lunch his mother had prepared he was good for food till at least the evening. Once there he could get lodgings in a pub or guest house. He had decided to travel in his uniform; it had a habit of opening doors and striking up conversations with the most unlikely of people, especially in small towns and villages.

By two o'clock in the afternoon he had arrived in London, the advice he had received from the ticket clerk was once in London head for Waterloo station. From there he could get a local train towards Portsmouth and then he was on his own. It sounded like as good a plan as any. After more wrong turns than he could count, he finally reached Waterloo. The station was heaving with soldiers, some going home, some re-joining their regiments and some standing around apparently not knowing where to go. Ernie fell into the last category.

'You alright there young man?' said an elderly gentleman in a railwayman's uniform.

'Not really,' said Ernie, 'I'm trying to get a train towards Bordon in Hampshire.'

'Right,' said the old fella, 'you based there or going home?'

'Neither, I'm looking for my wife, we got separated. She's a nurse and I'm told there are quite a few military hospitals round that way.'

'Well I don't know about the hospitals, but I can help you get the right ticket and platform.'

'That would be really appreciated.'

Ernie put out his hand, 'The name's Ernie, Ernie White.'

'Pleased to meet you Ernie, Tom Jackson,' they shook hands, 'Follow me and we'll get you on your way.' Ten minutes later Ernie had purchased a one way ticket to Portsmouth Harbour and was heading towards platform eight. The train was due to leave in ten minutes, so Ernie quickened his pace. The railwayman had told him to get off the train at Liphook, as he knew it was the closest station on route to Bordon, then it was up to Ernie to take it from there. Considering its destination, the train was very quiet. Ernie found an empty compartment, ate his lunch, then settled down to try and sleep for an hour or so. When Ernie arrived at Liphook, with the exception of the station master, it was deserted. As he stepped out onto the road he looked left and then right, took a deep breath and said out loud, 'Here we go then.'

Eventually Ernie arrived at Bordon. Being a garrison town there was a large military presence there. They directed him to one or two Red Cross establishments, but each time he drew a blank. For three days Ernie walked, thumbed lifts and asked local people if anyone had seen Ruth, but his efforts were futile. Only one thing left to do, head home and put his faith in the authorities. It was early evening and the chances of getting back to London that night were slim. As he retraced his steps he went through Passfield. He knew Liphook was much too far away for him to walk to before dark and even if he got a lift he would have to sleep on a bench in the station. Best bet was to find lodging in a pub or B&B, and set off first thing after a good breakfast. Set back off the road Ernie spotted a pub called The Fox. It looked a little neglected but any port in a storm as they say, and if they did have a room it was only for one night. Tired and disheartened Ernie went inside. At one end of the bar sat two old gentlemen with the dregs of a pint in front of each of them, probably been there with the same drink since the pub opened. They both looked up at Ernie, who nodded; they returned the gesture. From behind the bar a man stood up, by the look of him he was drinking more beer than his customers. His ruddy look and rotund waistline were a heart attack waiting to happen.

'Evening, can I help you?'

'Pint of best please.' said Ernie putting his bag by his feet.

'Coming right up.' said the barman, taking a glass from under the counter he started to pull Ernie his pint. 'Haven't seen you in these parts before.'

'No, I haven't been back long, been looking for my wife, we got separated in Germany. Her name's Ruth White, it was Zimmerman. She's a Jewish girl, a nurse.' The barman looked up as he placed Ernie a pint in front of him, 'Had it bad them Jewish folks, or so I'm told, the bloody SS are to blame.' Ernie made no reply, they may have been involved with the concentration camps, but those Ernie had crossed swords with were highly professional soldiers. His mind then flashed back to the battle in the barn. His section of men was amongst the finest fighting men he had ever seen. Big Jack Hawton and Geordie Mills, he was beginning to think they were invincible. But like so many before them, when the battle was raging, anything can happen.

'Have that one on me,' said the barman. Ernie thanked him and picked up the pint and took a long satisfying slug. Placing the glass back on the bar, Ernie asked, 'Have you got a room for the night?'

'Always got a bed for a soldier in this pub. Just one night is it?'

'Yes,' replied Ernie, 'got an early start in the morning. Back to my parents and then back to the grind. When I get a few more days off I'll do a bit more searching. But I'm beginning to wonder if she even made it across the channel.'

'Yes,' said the barman, 'lots of people have got split up over the last few years.'

Again Ernie took a drink from his pint, 'Did you say she was a nurse?' Ernie looked up.

'Yes, blonde girl speaks really good English, her name's Ruth.'

'I'm not saying I've seen her, but there is a Red Cross place a couple of miles down the Hollywater Road. Lady Pilkington turned half the old stately home into some sort of convalescence hospital for traumatised soldiers. Lord Pilkington was killed about two years back. Accidently shot by his own people so we heard, can you believe it?'

'Which way is that?' said Ernie.

'First on your right out of the village. If you head towards Bramshott you can't miss it, about two miles.'

Ernie stood up and grabbed his bag, 'Thank you,' he said to the barman and hurriedly left the pub leaving the door open behind him.

The barman shouted after him, 'Do you still want that room?' Ernie didn't reply, his mind completely focused on his task. He ran down the road, trying his best to ignore the constant niggling pain in his thigh and ankle. It wasn't long before he came to the junction the barman had told him to take. Undeterred by the thought of another two miles of pain he set off down the lane. The best part of half an hour later he saw the gates to what must have been the stately home. Some way off down a long drive he could see the large house. On the surrounding lawns were marquees with red crosses dotted about. A line of half a dozen makeshift ambulances was confirmation this was the place. Composing himself he set off down the drive. The lawns were bustling with people. As he got closer in between two of the marquees, he saw a group of girls all in nursing uniforms were sat on the lawns, some smoking some just taking a well-earned break. Ernie strolled over to them, 'Excuse me ladies,' they all turned as one to look at him. A very attractive brunette said, 'Hello soldier, you here for me?' they all laughed.

Ernie smiled back at her, 'Not today. I'm looking for a girl.'

'You aren't the first bloke I've heard say that,' again they all laughed.

Ernie felt himself blush, he was outnumbered and outwitted.

'No, seriously,' said Ernie, 'Her name is Ruth White, she's a Jewish girl, might be using the name Zimmerman, blonde hair.' Before he finished her description one of the girls said, 'That sounds like the new girl, got here about a week ago. She's working in the house.'

Ernie's face lit up, he thanked her and walked towards the main house.

One of the girls shouted after him, 'If it's not her I'll still be here.'

Still walking Ernie turned and raised a hand in acknowledgment. Ernie could feel his heart starting to race. Was it her? In front of the house were large stone steps, which lead to a huge double fronted door. The doors were held open by two thick ropes, attached to the wall by two highly polished brass hooks. He stopped to compose himself. Slowly he took two large breaths, then walked in. The downstairs rooms had been turned into small bedrooms consisting of anything from four to six beds. One by one Ernie peered into the rooms hoping the next one would contain the familiar face of his wife. There were a number of nurses milling around doing various jobs, but none even resembled her. The stairs in the main hall split into two going up to a large gallery style landing. Ernie made his way up the stairs. At the top he looked left and then right, there was a wing on either side. Randomly he turned left and started walking, it was the biggest house he had ever seen. There must have been at least ten bedrooms on the left wing alone, assuming they were bedrooms. He was about halfway down the hall when a door a few yards ahead on his right opened.

A regal looking middle aged woman stepped out and closed the door behind her, it was Lady Pilkington. Ernie stopped 'Can I help you?'

'I'm not sure,' said Ernie, 'I'm looking for a girl I met in Germany, I thought she might be working here, she's a nurse.'

'These are my family's private quarters; we only opened up downstairs to the Red Cross.'

'I'm very sorry,' said Ernie, 'I'll leave.' Ernie turned and walked back towards the stairs.

'One second young man.'

Ernie turned round, 'What's the name of the girl you're looking for?'

'Ruth,' said Ernie, 'Ruth White, but she may be using the surname Zimmerman.'

The woman smiled, 'Let me guess, your name is Ernest?' 'Well I prefer Ernie, but how did you know?' Suddenly the penny dropped, as Ernie smiled, a tear trickled out the corner of his already damp eyes. Quickly he wiped it away.

'Follow me.' she said. Ernie followed the women down the stairs through to the back of the house, down some more stairs and into a large very busy kitchen.

With her back to them sat sipping a cup of tea was Ruth. She was oblivious to his presence. Lady Pilkington just pointed and smiled. Keeping very quiet Ernie walked up behind her, stopping a few steps away.

'Didn't think you were going to get away that easy did you?' Ruth froze. Feeling her heart miss a beat she took a deep breath and put her cup down on the table. Slowly she stood up and turned round. As the tears ran down her face Ernie said, 'Told you I would find you.' Simultaneously they stepped forward and embraced. Ruth flung her arms around his neck and Ernie firmly held her waist. He lifted her off the ground and spun her around to a rapturous applause from everyone in the kitchen.

Through tears of joy she said, 'I love you Ernie White!'

'Likewise,' said Ernie. Placing her back on her feet, they kissed.

The old veteran looked up through tear-filled eyes and said, 'and that was that. I took her home the next day to meet my parents, they thought she was wonderful. We got all the paperwork sorted out confirming we were married, it took a while but it all sorted itself out in the end. When my brothers came home we had a family get together, nothing too big, just a few relatives round, meet the family type of thing. I had to go back to my regiment, the wife stayed at my parent's house till we got married quarters. Got a position working in the stores after the war, due to me leg and all that.' With a disgruntled look he continued, 'Weren't for me, stuck it as long as I could, indoors all the time pen pushing. Ruth wanted to start a family so I decided to call it a day.'

With a sombre look on his face he said, 'Over fifty years we were married before I lost her. In all them years I don't remember us having a cross word. When you experience such hard times as them you appreciate what you've got, there's more to life than money and material things. Enjoy time with the wife and kids, have good holidays together because before you know what's what, you'll wonder where all the time has gone. Take my advice Alex, live every day like it's your last.'

'I'll remember that old pal,' said Alex, sitting up straight on his chair. 'You should write a book.'

Ernie had a little chuckle to himself, 'I don't think they would believe me.'

'Alright Dad,' called Ernie's son Steve, appearing out of nowhere, his two young sons in tow close behind, playfully thumping each other. Startled by his appearance Ernie looked up. 'Alright son, is that the time already?'

'What do they say Dad? Time flies when you're having fun.' The two young boys were getting a little rowdy. Steve turned round, 'Pack it in you pair, or you'll get it when you get home.' 'They're alright, leave them be son, couple of rabbits. This is Alex, we've been having a chat; he's an ex-serviceman.'

'Pleased to meet you Alex,' said Steve offering him his hand. 'Has he been telling you all his old war stories?'

'And some,' said Alex smiling.

Steve looked over at the poppy boxes, now neatly stacked under the table. 'Christ you've sold the bloody lot!' Ernie looked into the box on the table, then under the table. 'I think you've broken the record Dad,' Ernie nodded. After all the memories that had been brought to the forefront of his mind; suddenly the record wasn't that important.

'Suppose we should clear up,' said the old veteran, pleased with the day's labours. Alex stood up and extended his hand to Ernie. 'Thanks for a great afternoon, I really enjoyed listening.' 'You're welcome,' said Ernie, 'it's nice to have someone to chat to especially about the old days.'

'Till next year,' said Alex. Ernie just grinned.

'Maybe,' he said under his breath, 'maybe.'

The End